"You brought me ~~here, Jake. You got~~ **me into this. Now** ~~you've got to get~~ **out."**

He opened his mouth to protest, studied her for a moment, then he sat down and huffed out a huge sigh.

"I'm only the Haven's handyman, Gem," he said weakly.

"You're the fixer—that's why all those people called you. Now help me figure out how to fix things for this child that my husband loved so dearly, when I can't even remember my own name. Wait a minute. That picture."

"Gem, are you okay? You look…weird."

"The picture that was in my wallet. That must be Alexa." Suddenly the sun felt too hot, the problems too large, the decisions too overwhelming. Somewhere in the recesses of her brain she thought she could hear a man's voice calling. *Take care of her. Take care of Alexa.*

The world wobbled. Had she really heard that, or was she dreaming? She felt so strange.

"Jake?" she whispered.

"Yes, Gem?"

"Have I ever fainted before?" Gemma didn't hear his reply as she slid off her chair onto the patio.

Lois Richer loves traveling, swimming and quilting, but mostly she loves writing stories that show God's boundless love for His precious children. As she says, "His love never changes or gives up. It's always waiting for me. My stories feature imperfect characters learning that love doesn't mean attaining perfection. Love is about keeping on keeping on." You can contact Lois via email, loisricher@gmail.com, or on Facebook (loisricherauthor).

Books by Lois Richer

Love Inspired

Rocky Mountain Haven

Meant-to-Be Baby
Mistletoe Twins
Rocky Mountain Daddy
Rocky Mountain Memories

Wranglers Ranch

The Rancher's Family Wish
Her Christmas Family Wish
The Cowboy's Easter Family Wish
The Twins' Family Wish

Family Ties

A Dad for Her Twins
Rancher Daddy
Gift-Wrapped Family
Accidental Dad

Visit the Author Profile page at Harlequin.com for more titles.

Rocky Mountain Memories

Lois Richer

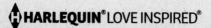
HARLEQUIN® LOVE INSPIRED®

LOVE INSPIRED BOOKS

Recycling programs
for this product may
not exist in your area.

ISBN-13: 978-1-335-42897-4

Rocky Mountain Memories

And we know that all things work together for good to them that love God, to them who are the called according to his purpose.

For whom he did foreknow,
he also did predestinate to be conformed
to the image of his Son, that he might be
the firstborn among many brethren.
—*Romans* 8:28–29

This book is dedicated to those who strive tirelessly to make a difference in their world. Shut out the naysayers, the negativity and the nonsense. Keep on keeping on. It's worth it.

Chapter One

He would have recognized her anywhere.

Oblivious to the May long weekend crowds thronging the Canadian airport in Edmonton, Jake Elliot strode directly toward Gemma Andrews, her gorgeous, waist-length tumble of auburn hair drawing him like a homing beacon.

"Hello, Gem," he said when he reached her. "Welcome home."

Her forest green eyes widened as she surveyed him, studying him as though he was a complete stranger.

"Uh, thank you." The lack of energy in her response bothered Jake.

"Are you all right?" He glanced at the strip of gauze covering her left temple. "Your head…?"

"Wh-who are you?" The pure panic in her words floored Jake.

"Excuse me." Only then did Jake notice Gemma's companion. "I'm Celia Shane from the Canadian embassy in Lima. You are?"

Unease skittered across his nerves. An embassy official had escorted Gem? Because she couldn't manage the trip on her own or…?

"Jake Elliot. I'm here to take Gemma home."

"I was told someone, um, older would meet us." Celia's phone pinged. She checked it and returned a text. "Apparently there's been a change. May I see some credentials?"

Jake fumbled for his wallet to show her his driver's license.

"Thanks. Hello, Jake." Celia's calm demeanor offered some serenity to Jake's whirling thoughts and apparently to Gemma, too, because her scared look eased. "Now, let me explain. As we notified the family, Gemma was at Machu Picchu with a tour group when the earthquake occurred. Subsequent to that notification, we learned she'd been struck by tumbling rocks, had fallen and, as a result of that, she's lost her memory. Because her head injury was minor and she's otherwise in good health, the hospital released her. They feel she'll recover best at home. Besides, they need the beds."

"Lost her memory?" Jake was stuck on that.

"Temporarily." Celia smiled. "Her doctors are convinced her memory will return in time."

"Will she—?"

"You two do know I'm standing here, right?" Gemma interrupted indignantly. "I *can* speak for myself."

Ah, that was more like the feisty woman Jake had known.

"Sorry, Gemma." Celia smiled at her. "Hazard of the job. I tend to take over."

"I am fine." Gemma's eyes met Jake's with the same directness she'd always employed. "I have a cut on my forehead and my brain is a little dinged up, but as Celia said, supposedly things will return to normal soon. In the meantime, I'm sorry but I don't know you."

"Sure you do. I'm Jake, your foster aunts' handyman." To his dismay, even that brought no flicker of recognition to her lovely green eyes.

"My *foster* aunts?" She studied him curiously. "Not my parents or my family?"

"They *are* your family, Gem." He hesitated, but maybe more information would reassure her. "Some years ago Tillie and Margaret Spenser brought you and three other foster girls to their home, The Haven, in the foothills of the Canadian Rockies."

"Um, okay." Gemma's blank look remained so Jake pressed on.

"Your sister Victoria lives at The Haven

permanently, with her husband and family, and the aunts, of course. Your sister Adele and her husband and kids live next door, while your other sister Olivia and her husband and family live on a nearby acreage." Still no comprehension. Jake added a little desperately, "They can all hardly wait to see you again."

"You've known me for a while?" she murmured, her expression pensive.

"I came to The Haven six years ago when you were seventeen. I've been there ever since." Jake caught Celia checking her watch. "You need to leave?"

"That text said I'm to fly to Ottawa in an hour to accompany someone back to Peru." She glanced at Gemma. "If you're all right?"

"She will be as soon as I get her home." Jake glanced around. He saw only a battered backpack and a small duffel. "Luggage?"

"Duffel's mine. The other is hers." Celia indicated the battered canvas with its multiplicity of stickers. "Authorities found it at the site. The hotel where Gemma and—where she was staying was flattened."

Gemma and Kurt. That's what Celia had been going to say. Why had she pulled back?

"The embassy will be certain to forward anything else they recover." She touched Gemma's arm. "Is it okay for me to leave you with Jake?"

"You have to go. You need to do your job, help someone else. I understand." Clearly summoning her pluck, Gemma thrust back her narrow shoulders.

Jake noted the thin cotton shirt she wore was far too large for her lithe frame and not at all her usual style. Well, it hadn't been, but things changed. Then her smile faltered and he forgot about what she wore as compassion for her suffering welled.

"You're going to be fine, Gemma." Celia must have sensed her uncertainty, too.

"Yes, I'm sure I will be." She cast him a sideways glance. "With Jake."

He didn't think Gemma looked or sounded

fine. She appeared nervous and uncertain, but in these circumstances, who wouldn't? Though Jake had wished many times for God to blank out the horror of his own past, he couldn't begin to imagine how it must feel to have forgotten everyone and everything. It would take time for Gem to feel secure again.

"You'll feel better once you're home." He hoped she could relax. "It's a long drive to The Haven. If you need to make a stop here, get some coffee or lunch, we'd best do that before we leave."

"All I want is to freshen up. The flight was long and tiring." She automatically headed for the ladies' room, as if she'd done it a hundred times before.

"How did she know where to go?" He stared at her retreating figure.

"Some things she does from rote. I guess that part of her memory is intact. Recent events are a blank though." Celia shrugged. "She can recite tons of information about lots of different locales she's taken tours to, but she can't tell you anything about the earthquake, what happened before or after it, or her personal past. Which reminds me, I need to talk to you before she returns."

"Okay."

"Gemma doesn't remember that she was married," Celia warned in a low voice. "She doesn't remember Kurt at all."

"How could she forget her own husband?"

"It's part of her injury, I guess." Celia shrugged. "Anyway, you need to be aware that she also has no idea that he died in the earthquake. My office contacted her family as soon as they found out, but apparently you'd already left to come here. I didn't feel it was my place to tell her," the woman explained.

"Why not?" he asked, brow furrowed.

"I couldn't gauge what her response might be. I was worried that if she reacted badly, there wouldn't be anyone to support her." Celia chewed her bottom lip. "Of course, hearing of Kurt's death might trigger her memories, too. Either way, I believe she needs someone who knew them both to help her through her loss and grief. The important thing, according to her doctors, is that with her type of brain injury, the fastest way to recovery is no stress."

"You want me to tell her." Jake's heart sank as he read between the lines. "You don't think her aunts should do it?"

"It's your decision, of course, but I do think it should be you, for several reasons." Celia frowned. "Gemma will find it difficult enough to deal with the family she doesn't remember. Four sisters, aunts, nieces and nephews. It's a lot. I believe it would be simpler for her if she'd already faced the complication of her husband's death when she meets her family."

Inwardly Jake groaned. How was he supposed to tell Gem that Kurt, the man she'd loved and married less than a year ago, was gone?

"Mostly I believe you should do it because

you're her friend, her very good friend.
Aren't you?" Celia seemed pleased by his
nod. "Excellent. To regain her memories,
Gemma's going to need someone she can
lean on, depend on and talk to without worrying about offending them. I think that's
you, Jake. Perhaps during the journey home,
you can work it in that she's now a widow.
I—" She stopped. "Here she comes."

*Work it in? Like, "By the way, Gem, no-
body told you but you're now a widow?"*
Jake's brain scoffed.

He stood by Celia, watching Gemma stride
toward them. She moved easily across the
space, making her appear confident and assured. Though appreciative heads turned to
admire her beauty, Gemma appeared unaware of the attention. Her intense gaze
rested on them.

"I'm ready to go," she announced, though
there was the faintest wobble in the words
and her eyes were red. "Thank you for ev-

erything, Celia. I appreciate your assistance so much."

"It was my absolute pleasure, Gemma." Celia hugged her, a trace of her own tears showing. "I put my card in your pack so that we can keep in touch. I want to know how you're doing. If you need anything," she added as she drew away, "anything at all, you let me know and I'll try to help. Maybe one day you'll return to Peru and we'll have lunch together. *Adiós o hasta pronto, mi querido amigo.*"

"Hasta que nos encontremos de nuevo," Gemma responded in a very quiet tone.

Jake blinked at her automatic Spanish rejoinder before remembering Gemma was fluent in several languages. Another reason why becoming a tour guide had seemed so perfect for her.

Celia waved, picked up her duffel and hurried away. Gemma watched her leave as though she was losing her best friend.

"Things will get better, Gem," he reassured her, trying to sound cheerful.

"Promise?" She gave him a half-hearted smile and then slung her pack over one shoulder. "I have a hunch they're going to get much worse first. I'm ready. I guess."

Jake had never heard Gemma sound so uncertain. She'd always been full of confidence and assurance.

Had been.

"I could take that—" He immediately choked back his offer to carry her backpack when her chin lifted and she glared at him. "Right. Let's go." He pulled his keys out of his pocket as they walked toward the exit. Outside in the clear sunlight he hesitated, concerns rising at her fragile appearance. "It's quite a hike to the car."

"Do you know me well, Jake?" Gemma's green eyes challenged him.

"Pretty well," he said. *Not that well*, his brain rebuked. *You never thought she'd elope.* "You've been away for a while, but I used to," he clarified.

"If you know me at all, then you know that I can quite easily manage a little walk across a parking lot. Right?" One auburn eyebrow arched imperiously.

"But you've been—right." He stifled his objection and pointed. "I'm parked over that way."

Gemma walked beside him, her head swiveling from right to left, taking in the sights of fully leafed trees scattered here and there, and the sound of chirping birds. "It's summertime." She sounded surprised.

"Late May. Springtime in North America and not quite summer in the Rockies," he explained. "The days are much longer but remember our nights are still chilly."

"That's the thing—I don't remember." She sighed. "So many things I've forgotten."

"So many things to rediscover now that you're home." As they reached her foster aunts' big, roomy SUV, Jake hit the unlock button and opened her door.

His phone dinged with a text which he ignored. Someone needing his help, no doubt. The community had gotten in the habit of calling on him for aid with lots of things, but he was busy helping Gemma right now and she came first. He waited until she was comfortably seated with her backpack on the floor, before he closed her door and took his own seat.

"It's not going to be a fast trip out of the city," he warned.

"Rush hour in Edmonton is never fast." Gemma blinked. "I have no idea how I know that," she muttered. "Actually, I'm not sure about a whole lot of things. I know what they told me, but I can't recall any personal details, like my birthday or when I started leading tour groups or—anything."

"I can tell you a little," Jake offered. "After you graduated from high school, you studied languages. You were always good at French in school."

"Le printemps à Paris est le meilleur moment pour visiter," Gemma murmured. Her eyes flared with surprise. "Uh—"

"See? Your memory is there, Gem. It just needs to wake up." He grinned at her as they sat at a red light.

"But why do I remember that when I can't remember my own name or where I live?" She sounded irritated. "Or these aunts you mentioned. Or the sisters. Or this haven place."

"You'll love The Haven. It's a big old stone manor house perched on the top of a hill with the most wonderful view of the valley and in the distance, the Rockies. It's surrounded by untouched forest." He felt the intensity of her focus on him. "That's what makes it such a perfect place for your aunts' ministries."

"Ministries?" She blinked. "Like they lead a church there or something?"

"No." Jake chuckled. "The ladies have faith—very strong faith—in God. They spent years as missionaries in Africa. Now they're using their home and land as a place for troubled foster kids to come for respite. Your sisters run the programs for them."

"How old are these aunts?" Gemma asked.

"Seventy-six, but you'd never know it. They are very active and extremely involved in their community. I doubt Tillie and Margaret Spenser will ever truly retire because they love helping people." Jake paused before adding, "I should know. They saved my life."

"I'd like to hear that story." Gemma pressed back against the seat, as if she was finally comfortable with him.

"Maybe some other time," he said, trying to gird himself for adding to her pain. "First there's something I need to discuss with you."

The serious note in Jake's voice warned Gemma that whatever he wanted to talk about would not be pleasant. Internal warning signs flared. She was so weary of bracing herself for the unknown. Yet what alternative did she have?

Just then Jake's phone rang. She waited while he answered it.

"Hey, Marv," he said after pressing a button on the dashboard.

"Hate to bother you, Jake, but I'm at Gerda Brown's place, trying to fix her water heater. Except it can't be done. The thing's finished and she can't afford a new one. I already used the spare one you found at O'Shea's place for someone else last month. Any ideas?"

"I'm tied up at the moment, Marv. Why don't you go pick up one at the hardware store? Put it on my tab. I'll figure it out later." After a few moments he ended the call. "Sorry about that."

"You're buying a water heater for somebody who can't afford one?" When he nodded, she asked, "Why?"

"Because they need it." He shrugged his

wide shoulders as if it didn't matter. "Anyway, as I was saying. I need to tell you—" His phone rang again and then a third time. His lips pursed but he didn't answer either call. When Gemma tilted an eyebrow at him, his face reddened and he muttered, "They can wait till I get back."

She giggled when the phone rang again. "Maybe not."

"It's from three different callers. Probably three different issues." Jake sounded impatient. She guessed he wanted to say whatever was on his mind.

"I'm listening." She shifted when he didn't immediately speak. "Tell me what you need to, Jake."

"It's sad news, actually." He licked his lips and then pressed them together. "You were married, Gem. To Kurt Andrews. You eloped about eight months ago."

The way he said it, in short staccato bursts, revealed his distress in telling her. But she didn't feel distressed. She felt…empty? The yawning unknown threatened to overwhelm her until she looked at Jake, and some part of her brain calmed. He was a nice guy who bought water heaters for needy women. He'd probably been pressed into duty on her behalf, though he obviously wasn't comfortable with explaining this. She touched his arm.

"Just tell me," she murmured. "Then I can deal with it."

"Kurt was killed in the earthquake." Jake huffed out a breath. "I'm sorry, Gem. I don't have any details. Celia only told me that the embassy is certain he did not survive."

"Oh." Gemma frowned. It didn't feel as if they were talking about anyone she knew, let alone a husband. What did it mean? "Does his family know? Will I have to tell them?"

"You are his family, Gem. His parents died in a car accident just after you were married." Free of the crush of traffic and now on the divided highway, Jake accelerated.

"No siblings?" Gemma mused, struggling to sort through her building questions.

"You are Kurt's only remaining family."
Jake frowned when she didn't immediately
respond. "Are you all right?"

"Actually, no." Gemma couldn't control
her burst of irritation. "I was married less
than a year to a man I loved?" She glanced at
Jake, relieved to see his firm nod. "I was his
wife, yet I feel blank. I'm sad that he died,
of course, but it doesn't feel *personal*. Isn't
that shameful?"

"No. It's part of your injury. Truthfully,
I'm sort of relieved you don't remember him
yet," Jake said, a hint of sternness coloring
his voice. He looked embarrassed by his ad-
mission.

"You are? Why?" Gemma's curiosity about
this unusual man grew.

"Because you're going to need your
strength to deal with your living family,"
he told her, his voice very gentle. "Mourning will come later."

"Did you know Kurt?" Gemma sensed
something in Jake's responses that didn't jibe

with her impression of him as open and honest. It felt like he was hiding something.

"I knew Kurt the same length of time as I've known you. He was a local, born and raised in Chokecherry Hollow, that's the town near your foster aunts' home." He shrugged. "I liked him a lot and I know he loved you very much."

"Oh." There were a hundred questions roiling inside her head, but suddenly Gemma didn't want to ask them. She needed time to absorb the fact that she had been a wife— and was now a widow.

To escape the miasma of her whirling brain, she retrieved her backpack. She knew her passport was tucked into the exterior zippered pocket because she'd put it there. She saw Celia's card there, too. But she'd been too tired and too muddled to open the pack that had been handed to her right before she'd left the hospital.

Now curious about what might lie inside, she unzipped the main cavity and began withdrawing the contents. A wallet of soft white leather came first. A driver's license tucked under clear plastic revealed her own face staring back at her. She looked so happy. Behind it was a small snapshot of her and a blond-haired, blue-eyed man.

"Is this Kurt?" She held the photo so Jake could see.

"Yes." A muscle flickered in his jaw. "He's—he was very attractive. You two looked good together."

Gemma didn't respond. She was too busy staring at another photo that was partially stuck to the back of Kurt's, as if the wallet and pictures had been damp. A little girl, also blonde, also blue-eyed, gazed back at her. She wore a fancy dress like children wear at Christmas or on their birthdays. Perhaps four or five, she appeared happy as she clutched a small brown teddy bear and grinned at the camera as if it was her best friend.

"Do you know who this is?" She held up the photo.

"No. I've never seen her before." Jake glanced at her before suggesting, "A foster child you adopted maybe? You used to support several."

It was a good guess, but it didn't feel right to Gemma. Since she had no idea why, she set the photo on the console between them while she checked out the rest of the contents in her backpack, including a metal tag with her name embossed on it. *Gemma Andrews, Tour Director, WorldWide Tours.* It bore deep scratches.

"I think I was wearing this when they found me," she murmured, her fingers tracing the marks. "I have a bruise this shape near my shoulder…"

A memory flickered on the fringes of her subconscious. People gathered around her, laughing as she told them a story, but she couldn't quite recall the entire memory.

"That tag is probably how they identified you. Anything else that's interesting in there?" Jake asked.

"A sweater." She drew out the lime-green cardigan and fingered the soft wool. "Alpaca. I'm guessing I got this at Arequipa. That's where you find the best alpaca garments." The words spilled out spontaneously, shocking her.

"Did you often take your tour groups there?" Jake's question shook off her surprise.

"Usually. They always gave our guests these wonderful gift packs of Peruvian coffee" Gemma stared at him. "Hey, I remembered that and I didn't even try."

"Perhaps that's the way it's going to be," Jake murmured. "The less you strive to think about it, the more relaxed your brain will be, and you'll recover quickly."

"Maybe." It sounded good, but Gemma couldn't shake an ominous sense that things were going to get a lot tougher. She replaced everything in the pack, except the sweater which she pulled on, and the picture. The little girl's joyful face gazed back at her. "She looks so happy, as if she loves whomever she's looking at." A wave of wistfulness swamped her.

What was it like to feel so loved? To love someone and know they loved you? Frustrated by her inability to recall anything personal, Gemma tucked the photo into her pocket while she searched for a topic of conversation. Jake beat her to it.

"You must be wondering why I came to get you instead of your family. Your aunts intended to come, as if anything could have stopped them."

"They're not here and you are, so something must have," she pointed out.

"True, though I would have driven them anyway because Margaret—well, let's say city driving's not her thing." He chuckled.

"So they changed their minds." Gemma shrugged. "It doesn't matter."

"No, they didn't change their minds. Tillie woke up with a sore throat and a fever." Jake paused to ask if she wanted to stop for anything. When Gemma declined, he continued. "Margaret intended to come until a guest showed up unexpectedly, a military man she'd been corresponding with for some months. He was desperate to speak to her and she was worried about his mental state. She sends her apologies."

"Oh." Gemma didn't understand what he was talking about. Jake must have realized that because he explained.

"For years your aunts have conducted a letter-writing campaign to our overseas military troops to offer them encouragement, prayers and someone to talk to. The ladies have a huge list of correspondents." He shrugged. "When they get leave, those folks frequently come to The Haven for a visit, to talk to the ladies personally."

"I see." So her aunts had several ministries. Which didn't explain why one of her foster sisters hadn't come in their place.

Gemma had no sooner had the thought than Jake addressed it.

"Your sisters wanted to be here, too," he told her.

"But?" Was it wrong to feel disappointed that her family had sent their handyman to get her, even though Jake seemed a very nice man?

"Victoria's going through a difficult pregnancy. She struggles to deal with anything before eleven o'clock in the morning." Jake grimaced. "Best for her to be sick at home. Adele offered to take Margaret's place until she got an emergency request to foster two orphaned infants who'd just lost their parents. Olivia's in hospital because yesterday she gave birth to a brand-new baby daughter. So you're stuck with me."

"Not stuck," Gemma protested. "It's very kind of you to sacrifice your time—say, what exactly is it that you do at The Haven, Jake?" It felt strange to say those words, as if she should know. But Gemma couldn't form a mental picture of her family's home or his work.

"I do whatever your aunts need me to do." A muscle twitched in Jake's jaw. "I owe them big-time for saving my life, so fulfilling their needs is my job and my pleasure."

Saving his life.

Gemma was about to ask about that when she realized they were taking an exit off the highway. And his phone was ringing again.

"Sounds like somebody else needs you," she said.

"Apparently." He checked the number before letting it go to voice mail. "I don't think it's serious, but I'll get some coffee and call them back. I was up very early," he said, obviously aware of her curiosity. "How about you?"

"I don't mind stopping." She knew it was an excuse so he wouldn't have to say more about his past, but that didn't mean she intended to let the subject go.

Gemma was stymied by her reactions to

him. Why did she feel so comfortable with him? What was with this keen interest in Jake? And why did she feel compelled to discover why this strong, competent man would need two elderly women to save his life?

It was natural that she had a lot of questions about herself, important knowledge like who she was, where she'd grown up, her childhood, her foster aunts and sisters, especially her husband. She couldn't remember any of that. What kind of a woman forgot her own wedding?

But now Gemma also had growing questions about Jake Elliot. A good-looking man, he was tall, solidly built and radiated an empathetic aura of strength and confidence. Rather like a young John Wayne in a very old movie, though this handyman was definitely not old. He was probably close to her age, which was twenty-three according to her passport. He seemed perfectly comfortable in his well-fitting jeans, cotton shirt, cowboy boots and battered leather jacket, while his mussed brown hair and piercing blue eyes made him seem vibrantly alive, unlike the dull blankness that hung over her mind.

Besides all that, Jake was apparently the go-to guy for the community's needy folks.

A strange combination to be sure, though why he should intrigue her so was a puzzle Gemma couldn't fathom. The only thing she did know was that Jake wasn't like her. He knew exactly who he was, where he was going and, unlike her, exactly where he belonged.

It might take time, but she was determined to discover exactly who this poised, handsome handyman was behind the friendly, self-effacing smile.

And somehow she intended to learn why he had needed saving.

Chapter Two

Spurning an offer of coffee, Gemma elected to stretch her legs while Jake returned his calls. Tactfully, he deferred the concerns of each person, assuring them he'd handle their needs when he returned. By the time Gemma reappeared at the car, he'd come up with solutions to each problem presented. The outreaches he did were mostly busy work for his brain, but they helped suppress the barely buried memories of his past. That was exactly why he'd taken on the role of community problem-solver.

"Everything okay?" Gemma asked as she fastened her seat belt.

"Yep. Next stop, The Haven."

While he drove, Gemma slept. Every so often she would call out or startle and waken herself. Then her long, lush lashes would droop, and she'd doze again.

Jake had a thousand questions. Had she been happy with Kurt? Had marriage lived up to her expectations? Did she regret not having a big, fancy wedding? In the past she'd have told him all of that without his asking. He yearned to rebuild the old camaraderie they'd shared.

He was thinking about her too much. He needed to adjust his thoughts.

In six years of living at The Haven, this was one of a handful of times that Jake had left the place. Was that why he felt so antsy? At The Haven he could bury himself in other people's issues because there was little about the place to remind him of Lily or of the reason for her death. The folks at The Haven and in Chokecherry Hollow had become a bandage over the pain of his loss.

As Gemma now was?

I promise, Lily. I will never love another as I did you. I will never risk another woman's life through my selfishness. Never again. I promise.

He was Gemma's friend and he'd do whatever he could for her, but friendship was all they could ever share.

Jake switched on the radio for distraction, glad when he turned off the highway that Gemma would arrive home in daylight. It wasn't the Andes in autumn, but springtime in the Canadian Rockies *was* pretty spectacular.

"Time to wake up," he said when there were only a few minutes left in their trip. "You need to see this, Gem."

"I haven't done a thing and yet all I do is sleep." She sat up and rubbed her eyes, wincing when her fingers brushed the injury on her forehead. She yawned and stretched her neck, twisting and turning to get a good look at her surroundings. "Spectacular," she breathed.

"It is," Jake said with smug satisfaction, as if the land was his own. "We'll soon be home. Then you can climb into bed and really rest, if you want."

He wanted to ease her transition, but how could you help someone who couldn't remember anything about their past? Maybe he should have let her sleep.

"I've always loved the snowcaps on these mountains." She paused. "I mean, I think I have."

"You don't have to monitor every word. Just take it as it comes, Gem. And I know exactly how you feel." The serenity of the vast forest surrounding The Haven filled Jake's soul. He loved it here. This was *his* haven and he never wanted to leave, though technically it wasn't *his* home. He'd lost that the day—

Jake shoved away the guilt and drove uphill toward the big stone house where the aunts lived.

"Jake?" Gemma's voice came soft, breathless.

"Yeah." He glanced at her. Worried by her pallor, he pulled to the side of the road. "Feel sick?"

"Yes. What if I don't ever remember them?" She grabbed his arm and clung to it. "What if this never feels like home? I'm so scared."

"Don't be." He wrapped her icy fingers in his and held on to them, trying to ease her discomfort the way a movie hero would simply because Gemma—the old Gemma—had always admired white-knight heroes. "Everything is going to be fine. There's no rush about remembering. You'll do it when you're ready. No one will pressure you. Everyone will understand. All they care about is that you're home and unhurt—well, mostly unhurt," he corrected with a smile, wishing she'd lose that terrified expression.

"But—but—"

"Gem." He gave in to his longing to comfort her and slid his palm against her cheek for just a second. "You used to have a special verse you'd recite whenever you needed to encourage yourself. Do you remember it? It starts, 'God is our refuge and our strength.'" He removed his hand and waited for her to finish it.

"'A tested help in times of trouble.'" Eyes wide, she nodded. "I do remember that."

"Now think about the words," he suggested while his brain called him a hypocrite. *God hasn't been your refuge or strength, Jake. Not for years.*

She remained silent for a few moments before huffing a sigh.

"Okay. Guess I'm as ready as I'll ever be."

"Atta girl." He shifted into gear. "The Haven's gorgeous, isn't it? All that stonework with those towers and—" One glance at Gem's face and Jake cut off his commentary, sensing that she needed silence to gather her pluck for the reunion ahead.

He sent up a prayer for her, for strength and a calm spirit, and then wondered at himself. He didn't talk to God anymore. Hadn't since… Anyway, Gemma Andrews wasn't his responsibility.

Yet from the first day he'd arrived at The Haven, Jake had felt protective of her, as if he had to be there in case she needed him.

"There are so many of them!" Gemma gasped, drawing his attention to the house and the folks assembled on the driveway.

"Those aren't all your relatives," he sputtered, amused by her shocked expression. "I'm guessing your family arranged for whatever kids' group is visiting The Haven to form a welcoming committee. Relax," he chided as her fingers tightened around her seat belt. He parked, turned off the car and waited a moment before asking, "Ready?"

"As I'll ever be," she whispered. She lifted

her hand to open her door, pausing when Jake shook his head.

"Wait." He climbed out, strode to her side and offered a hand to help her exit the car. Her hair had loosened from the topknot she'd tied it in earlier and now tumbled past her waist. Her face was strained and the jeans she wore had seen better days.

But Jake thought she had never looked lovelier.

"Welcome home, Gemma," he said softly, and then he drew her forward to meet her family.

Gemma licked her lips as she mentally reminded herself, *They're my family.* My *family.*

She didn't feel like she belonged with them.

"Our dear, dear girl." One of the elderly women, an auntie perhaps, wrapped her in a gentle, fragrant embrace. She brushed a kiss against Gemma's brow before holding her back to examine her. "We are so thankful you're home, dear."

"I—er, I'm glad to be here," she whispered. It wasn't home—not yet—but how could a mere hug feel so wonderful? She glanced from one lady to the other. "You're twins!" Her face burned at the peals of laughter around her.

"Guess I forgot to tell you that, Gem. This is your Aunt Tillie," Jake explained.

"Hello. Jake said you were ill." As Gemma squeezed her hand she noticed the woman's red nose. "I hope you're feeling better."

"A simple case of the summer sniffles. Some people worry too much," Tillie said with a glare at her doppelganger.

"You are Aunt Margaret. It's very nice to—" Gemma had been going to say *meet you.* But that was hardly appropriate. "To be here," she finished.

"My dear, you should be resting in bed." Margaret wrapped tender arms around her in a second hug. "You've had a dreadful ordeal."

"I'm fine." Gemma had never felt more on show.

"Margaret tends to fuss," Tillie murmured.

"It's nice to be fussed over, but I'm truly all right." She wanted to get this over with. "Thank you for the welcome," she said, scanning the assembled group. One glance at Jake and he immediately understood. He nodded at someone and after the group of children had sung a welcome song they hurried away, apparently to other activities.

"These are your sisters, Gemma." He introduced each woman, her husband and her children.

Her foster sisters at least resembled the descriptions he'd given her during their long ride here. Their children's names would require memorizing.

"I should have brought gifts," Gemma whispered to Jake when the silence stretched too long.

"No, you shouldn't have, Gem," Victoria

said. "All we care about—all we've been praying for—is that you'd come home safely."

"I care about presents, Auntie Vic!" A little girl glared at her aunt until her mother—Adele?—hushed her. "Well, I like 'em," she muttered defiantly.

Gemma grinned at her. "I like presents, too," she said.

"We're so sad about Kurt, Gemmie." Olivia, a tiny baby snugged against her chest in some type of sack, embraced her. "I'm sorry you had to go through that alone."

"Thank you." *Go through? Oh, she means losing my husband. But I can't even remember what Kurt looked like, just as I can't remember any of you.* "Jake said your baby is brand-new," she murmured, staring at the delicate face and wondering if she'd ever wanted to be a mother. "Congratulations."

"Thanks. This is your niece, Mirella. She's pleased to meet you."

"Me, too, Mirella." Gemma stirred at the

touch on her shoulder. Jake. Her protector. When he smiled, her tension eased.

Thank You, God, for Jake. Funny how natural it seemed to pray. Was she very religious? How could she not *know* something like that?

As if sensing her confusion, Jake asked, "How about some lemonade on the deck, Gem?"

"Great idea! What's wrong with us, keeping our girl standing here?" Tillie smiled at Gemma before turning to Margaret. "Come, sister. Let's savor this blessing of having our four girls home once more. It's been forever, or so it seems."

"Thank you all for your warm welcome," Gemma repeated politely.

Her family—how strange that word felt— sat around her on a huge deck overlooking a picturesque valley. Everyone chattered at once. It should have sounded like bedlam, and yet to Gemma, the loving, teasing voices and laughing children who played boisterously nearby were a balm to her jumbled mind. With the warm sun on her face and several delicious cookies in her stomach, her eyelids soon drooped.

"Gem?" Tension underlaid Jake's husky drawl.

"Yes?" She blinked before forcing herself to sit up straight. "Did I fall asleep again? I'm so sorry," she apologized to the group who now stared at her with sympathy. "Is my hair a mess?" When she lifted her hand to smooth the strands she noticed an older man in a three-piece suit standing at the edge of the patio. "I'm sorry if I should know you," she began to apologize. She stopped when Jake's fingers squeezed her shoulder.

"Gemma, this is Wilber Hornby. He's a local lawyer." There was a graveness to Jake's tone that she didn't like. "He's here about Kurt."

"Now?" She frowned. "But I only just got here—"

"I'm very sorry," Mr. Hornby said in precise diction. "But Kurt was most insistent that if anything happened to him, I was to speak to you immediately. I promised I would do so, therefore I have come."

Only then did Gemma notice that, one by one, her family had silently left. Only her aunts, Jake and the lawyer remained with her. This must be serious. Funeral plans?

"O-okay." As she drained her glass of lemonade, she realized that Jake was about to depart, too. "Please stay?" she begged. "Please?"

Jake glanced at the aunts. They nodded. He appeared to consider something but finally shrugged and sat down. Gemma mouthed *thanks* before turning to face the sober-faced lawyer.

"What is this about?" she asked.

"It's about a girl," Mr. Hornby said. "Your husband's four-year-old stepdaughter. Her name is Alexa."

Gemma had steeled herself to hear something important, perhaps something about Kurt's final wishes or... Wait a minute.

"My husband was married before me?" She turned questioningly toward Jake and was astonished by his outraged glared at the lawyer.

"Kurt Andrews never had eyes for anyone but Gemma for as long as I knew him." Jake glowered at the lawyer. "He was always crazy in love with her. What are you saying?"

The way Jake said the words, fiercely, with his blue eyes glittering, jaw clenched and his back ramrod straight—it was as if this man was indignant on her behalf, Gemma thought wonderingly. That made her feel special, valued, precious.

"I have a letter from Mr. Andrews to his wife that will explain," Mr. Hornby began, drawing an envelope from his briefcase.

He held it out, but Gemma couldn't take it. She wasn't sure exactly why, only that she didn't want to have to deal with anything more right now, especially not a letter from a husband she couldn't remember.

"Can't it wait?" she begged, sending Jake a pleading look.

"Kurt's direction to me was to proceed as quickly as I could." The lawyer's set face told Gemma he would do his duty no matter what.

"Perhaps in this instance, Wilber," Aunt Tillie said softly, placing her hand on his arm, "we might dispense with her reading the letter right now. Couldn't you just tell Gemma the gist of it?" She glanced at her sister for support. "After all…"

The two women shared a look that told Gemma they knew, or at least guessed what was in that envelope.

"Those are not the terms—"

"I know, Wilber. And you've been most circumspect in coming here as soon as our dear girl arrived home," Margaret soothed. "But Gemma isn't herself. She's been through an earthquake and she has amnesia. The doctor's orders are for her to minimize stress."

Even Gemma could see the lawyer weakening under the genteel ladies' soft words and beseeching expressions. She had a hunch that there weren't many people who could deny these aunties whatever they asked for. They were characters. It would be fun to get to know them.

"If you could just explain to Gemma what you need from her, sir," Jake added quietly. "Once she knows whatever it is, she can think about it and come back to you if she needs clarification."

She threw him a grateful look. He was such a sweet man to always keep smoothing the way for her.

Always? Jake had smoothed her way before?

"Is that your wish, Mrs. Andrews?"

Gemma glanced around, wondering whom he was addressing and found everyone staring at her. Oh. *Mrs. Andrews.* That was *her* name. How strange.

"Gemma?" Mr. Hornby pressed.

"Yes, please. Just tell me the basics," she said, nodding.

"Very well, though it's rather difficult..." Mr. Hornby paused, gathered his thoughts and then began speaking. "Your husband— you remember he went to college after finishing high school?"

"I'm afraid I don't remember anything," Gemma told him. "Just pretend we never met before and tell me what you think I need to know about, um, Kurt."

"All right." Hornby cleared his throat. "He told me he was uncertain about his next step and went to college to try to figure things out. While he was there he met a woman, Anna, a law student in her final year, who became a good friend. Kurt learned she was pregnant and desperate to finish school. She felt she had no way to raise a child and adoption was out because she couldn't pay for a delay in her education. She intended to have an abortion."

"I see." *So the stepchild must be the Alexa he's talking about. But why would my husband...?*

"Kurt was totally against abortion. He said he tried desperately to talk Anna out of it, but she would not be swayed. She saw no other option." Hornby paused for breath, then continued. "To be brief, Kurt persuaded her to marry him, insisting he'd support her until the child was born and continue to work to ensure the child was cared for while Anna finished her schooling. Nothing romantic about it, Kurt said. His whole concern was for the child. Anna finally agreed to marry him on condition he told no one about their arrangement."

"Where was I during all this?" Gemma asked, struggling to absorb the information.

"Overseas, at language school," Jake said immediately. His face reddened at the surprised looks from the aunts. "I remember that's where you went after high school."

"You are correct, Jake. Gemma spent time mastering languages in Europe," Margaret agreed somberly.

Mr. Hornby cleared his throat.

"Please go on." A sudden chill made Gemma shiver. *Now what?*

"When the child, Alexa, was born, Kurt took care of her. He loved her, but he hated the secrecy of not being able to share her with his family. So after Anna graduated, Kurt came home one weekend to tell his parents the truth. When he returned, Anna and her child were gone." Mr. Hornby took off his glasses and polished them on his handkerchief.

"Gone where?" Gemma realized she was perched on the edge of her lawn chair. "And how do I fit in?"

"Anna later called Kurt to explain that she'd arranged for them to divorce. She had a new job and wanted a fresh start for herself and Alexa, and for Kurt. Anna was adamant that Kurt belonged with you. She'd always known he loved you." Mr. Hornby managed a smile.

"Easy for you to say," she muttered, a little embarrassed. It didn't seem like the lawyer was talking about anyone she knew.

"Mrs. Andrews, Kurt told me he loved you dearly and that there'd only ever been friendship between him and Anna." The lawyer's hard face softened. "But little Alexa had stolen a piece of his heart. Kurt had no legal or biological claim to her, of course. Still, he felt that if ever she needed him, as his mother had needed him, there should be funds available for her. That's why he set up her trust fund. His request was that if he was not able, you should manage the fund for Alexa. Kurt had great faith in your ability to protect her." He held up the letter. "This is his explanation to you about the matter."

"But why didn't he just tell me himself? Why did he keep it a secret?" Gemma's head ached as the knowledge whirled round and round inside it. The letter in her hand felt heavy, full of problems, and she already had too many of those. "What am I supposed to do with this fund? Make sure it's invested properly—something like that?" She glanced at Jake for help, but he appeared as puzzled as she felt. "I don't know anything about investing or trust funds."

Something clicked in her brain, like her words weren't quite true. But she didn't understand how that could be. And suddenly this world of everything unknown felt like it was closing in on her.

"May I say something, dear?" Tillie's soft voice broke through Gemma's confusion. "Margaret and I knew about Alexa. Kurt's parents confided in us."

"That was one of the reasons for the disagreement," Margaret chimed in.

"What disagreement?" Gemma read disapproval on the ladies' faces.

"My dear, you came home to announce

your elopement and we were very happy for both of you." Margaret's smile eased some of the tension gripping Gemma.

"But when we asked your husband privately if he'd told you about Alexa, he insisted that he wanted you to meet the child first so you could bond, but Anna and Alexa were away that weekend." Sadness edged Tillie's words. "We disagreed with Kurt's decision. We felt he should have explained about the child before you agreed to marry him. I'm afraid it caused a bit of a rift between us and him."

"He certainly should have told me the truth before we got married," Gemma said, feeling indignant for Kurt's wife. Wait, that was *her*! "But since he didn't, it's a moot point."

Everyone was watching her, including Jake. She shifted uncomfortably, waiting for someone to speak. When they didn't, she blurted out her thoughts.

"So what now? Am I supposed to do something about Alexa? Is she okay? And what in the world could I do anyway? I haven't even got a job." Worried and muddled, Gemma fumed. "I can't help myself, let alone a child."

"May I suggest something, Gem?" Jake's smile somehow calmed her. "Maybe you could find out about Alexa, make sure she and her mom are all right. At least then you'd have peace of mind."

"I guess I could do that," she agreed, then frowned. "What do I do after that?"

"If Alexa doesn't need Kurt's money, you could ensure it's wisely invested and then leave it to grow until she does need it," he said with a shrug.

"That sounds advisable," the lawyer agreed.

"Yes," Tillie said, though she was frowning. She looked at her sister.

"It does *sound* good. Only, Alexa and her mom aren't all right," Margaret blurted.

"How do you know that?" Jake studied the sisters with narrowed eyes.

"We've kept tabs on them. Kurt and Gemma were away so much, you see." Margaret cleared her throat. "We felt it our duty to watch over the child."

"And so?" Gemma replied automatically. She felt so confused and muddled and her headache was back.

"I'm sorry to tell you that Anna was accidentally killed three days ago in a drive-by shooting." Tillie's sad voice was hushed.

"The day of the earthquake," Gemma whispered, aghast.

"Yes." Margaret sighed. "Apparently Anna had a will that named Kurt as Alexa's guardian in the event of her own death. Because there are no other relatives and Kurt was unreachable, Anna's daughter, Alexa, was placed in foster care. We've been praying and praying for a way to help the child."

"Yes," Margaret exclaimed. "And now you're home, Gemma. A true answer to prayer."

"Me?" Gemma blinked. She glanced sideways at Jake and found no help in his shrug. So she studied her aunts. "I'm an answer to prayer? What am I supposed to do?"

"We have no idea, dear," Tillie said, her smile sweet.

"Not yet. But we'll think of something," Margaret said confidently. "We always do." She rose. "Or you will. Oh, dear, look at the time. I'm so sorry, Gemmie, but Tillie and I must leave. We have an appointment in Chokecherry Hollow that we simply cannot cancel, but it shouldn't take too long."

"My dear girl," Tillie said, rising and moving close to pat her shoulder. "You're safe now. Jake will show you around The Haven and your room is waiting for you. As always."

Gemma sat stunned as the ladies kissed her cheek and told her again how glad they were to have her home. Then they bustled away. The lawyer rose, too.

"I must also depart. As Kurt's executor, I'm happy to answer any questions you may have, Mrs. Andrews—Gemma. Call on me anytime." He, too, left.

Gemma felt like Dorothy in Oz, right after the tornado had touched down. Wait, how did she remember that?

"Well, I guess I'd better get started answering those calls—" Jake started to say.

"No you don't!" He was her lifeline and she wasn't about to let go of him in this sea of confusion. "You brought me here, Jake. You got me into this. Now help me figure it out."

He opened his mouth to protest, studied her for a moment and then poured himself another glass of lemonade. He sat down, huffed out a huge sigh and swallowed half of the pale yellow liquid.

"I'm only The Haven's handyman, Gem," he said weakly.

"You're the fixer, that's why all those people called you," she said, struggling to make sense of everything she'd learned. "Now help me figure out how to fix things for this child that my husband loved so dearly, when I can't even remember my own name. Wait a minute. That picture." She blinked, remembering the photo of the smiling child.

"Gem, are you okay? You look…weird."

"The picture that was in my wallet. That must be Alexa. Maybe Kurt did tell me about her and I just forgot. Along with everything else." Suddenly the sun felt too hot, the problems too large, the decisions too overwhelming. Somewhere in the recesses of her brain she thought she could hear a man's voice calling, *Take care of her. Take care of Alexa.*

The world wobbled. Had she really heard that or was she dreaming? She felt so strange.

"Jake?" she whispered.

"Yes, Gem?" His voice came from a long way away.

"Have I ever fainted before?" Gemma didn't hear his reply as she slid off her chair and onto the patio.

Chapter Three

For the next two days, Jake stayed away from The Haven, trying to catch up with his work and hoping to give Gemma time to absorb everything in her world. But with each day that passed, his concern about her ramped up. Somebody had to do something.

Though he'd called the local doctor after Gemma had fainted, though she'd been given a thorough checkup and she had pooh-poohed his concern, he worried. She did look and sound fine, yet she seemed somehow diminished. Apparently her interest in Alexa had also lapsed because she remained silent on that issue.

"Want to check out our fishing hole this afternoon?" Jake had asked yesterday when he'd seen her sitting on the deck. He'd pointed out the spot, expecting she'd jump at the chance to resume her favorite activity.

"I just showered. I'll get dirty scrabbling down that hill," she'd mumbled, barely meeting his gaze. "Anyway, Adele's a chef. She doesn't need me to bring home supper."

Excuses made, Gemma had resumed staring across the valley.

It seemed to Jake that she couldn't muster the strength to move on with her life. Since Tillie and Margaret gave the impression they were perfectly content to let their foster daughter float through the days, Jake felt it was up to him to help her snap out of it. Which was why when he found Gemma in the kitchen near noon today, still swathed in her bathrobe, he discarded his white-glove treatment.

"Since you're not busy, can you help me out?" He was relieved that his peremptory tone jarred her from her vacant stare through the massive window to the distant mountains.

"Help you out with what?" Though Gemma looked at him, her gaze was hazy, unfocused.

"With my work here at The Haven." It was the only thing he could think of to motivate her. "I'm behind."

"Because you took time off to come get me." As he'd expected, Gemma immediately jerked upright. Twin dots of color appeared in her cheeks. "I'm sorry, Jake. I've been selfish, haven't I?" She sounded more like herself. "I don't know that much about your work, or anything else for that matter. But I'll help however I can if you'll show me what to do."

"For starters, get dressed. Old clothes. We'll be working in the dirt." Jake lifted one eyebrow when she simply sat there. "Well?"

"Dressed. Got it." Gemma rose and strode across the room. When she reached the doorway, she stopped and turned. "Will you wait here, or should I find you?"

"I'm already late," he told her in a brusque tone that he despised but used because it seemed to be shocking her out of her dazed lethargy. "Find me in the garden."

"The garden." She didn't move. "Uh, the garden is...?"

He pointed.

"Right. I'll be there in five minutes," Gemma promised.

"Wear a sun hat," he called after her retreating form.

"Do you think that was wise, dear?" Tillie murmured.

Jake whirled to find the aunts standing behind him, both wearing disapproving frowns. They'd obviously overheard his less than gentle tone. Jake mentally grimaced, hating that he'd caused that look of strain on their sweet faces.

"Gemma needs to be busy, to be doing something," he explained gently. "Sitting around, waiting for her memory to return isn't helping her."

"What if it doesn't return?" Margaret's hushed tone revealed her concern.

"Ladies," Jake chided with a smile. "Where's your faith?" He was rewarded with their nods. "Until Gemma's memory returns, she needs a purpose. Maybe gardening will give her that." Did he sound more certain than he felt? "It's better than doing nothing," he offered belatedly.

"Yes, it is," Tillie agreed.

"Thank you for trying to help, Jake," Margaret added. "We've been afraid to push Gemma. Shame on us for our lack of faith in God."

"It's time we prayed about this in a different way, sister." Tillie slipped her hand in Margaret's arm and drew her out of the room. A moment later Gemma appeared clad in raggedy jeans, a T-shirt, a hoodie and a sun hat he hadn't seen for years.

"I thought you said you weren't waiting,"

she accused, her megawatt smile flashing. "The aunts," she guessed. "They waylaid me, too." She waved a piece of delicate pink notepaper.

"A Bible verse?" Jake guessed as he held the door for her to exit The Haven.

"Uh-huh." She handed it over so he could read the spidery script.

Whither shall I go from thy spirit? or whither shall I flee from thy presence? If I ascend up into heaven, thou art there: if I make my bed in hell, behold, thou art there. If I take the wings of the morning, and dwell in the uttermost parts of the sea; Even there shall thy hand lead me, and thy right hand shall hold me.

"Psalm 139." Jake handed back the note which Gemma folded and tucked into her back pocket.

"You know it?" She seemed surprised, yet her stride matched his and she never faltered.

"Sure, I know it." Jake hesitated to say more, but being Gemma, he figured she'd keep pressing for the why. "It's a good verse. I looked it up after someone said it to me once." He glanced her way and almost smiled at her raised eyebrows. She'd always been full of questions.

"Why did they quote that verse to you?"

"It was after a funeral." Two funerals, actually. *Change the subject, Jake.* "Did you think more about Kurt's stepdaughter?"

"Alexa. I haven't been able to think of anything else. I'm almost certain she's the child in that picture I found in my wallet. Maybe Kurt told me about her or maybe I found out." She shrugged. "Guess I'll never know."

"Either one sounds plausible." Relieved she hadn't brushed off the orphaned child, he asked, "Are you going to apply for her guardianship?"

"Me?" She gaped at him. "What do I know about kids? I was thinking more along the lines of bringing Alexa here for a visit. I've been watching the kids who come. They all seem to have a wonderful time."

"Yes." Jake had hoped for more, hoped for Gemma to interact with the child. Maybe if her focus wasn't on what she'd forgotten...

"You want me to weed?" Gemma stood at the fenced entrance to the garden, surveying it.

"Do you want to?" He smothered a laugh at her eager nod.

"Yes! I love weeding." As soon as the words were out, her forehead pleated. Her expression faltered. "Don't I?" she asked hesitantly.

"You did." He handed her a pair of work gloves she'd left behind long ago, and grinned as she slid them onto her slender fingers. "You've loved weeding ever since the first time the aunts sent you out to weed as punishment for some misdeed. You were supposed to work an hour. You were here for three and I didn't have to do it again for a week. You used to beg them to send you out to weed." He chuckled. "I often wondered if you sometimes broke a rule or misbehaved just so you could get your fingers in the dirt."

"Sounds like I was a brat." Gemma knelt and with a touch born of long experience, eased a thistle out of the ground from between tender carrot shoots. "Was that why I eloped, do you think, to break a rule?"

"I don't know the answer to that, Gem. You never said." Jake sank to his knees in the next row and began extricating the unwanted green invaders from around his beans.

Silence stretched between them, a comfortable peace The Haven always seemed to engender in him. At least it had until Gem's return. For some reason Jake now felt like he had to keep up his guard, had to keep reminding himself of his vow to Lily.

"There's something wonderful about weeding," Gemma murmured more to herself than him. "It's exciting, like you're preparing the way for something. You can't see exactly what's happening, but you know the end result will be so good. We'll have carrots." She said it almost triumphantly.

"And peas and beans and…" Jake let it trail away, amused by the satisfaction filling her face.

"I remember once when I was in Italy—" Gemma stopped, blinked and stared at him. "I remember something!"

"Good. What is it?" He kept on weeding, waiting to hear whatever thought was emerging. Listening to Gemma speak about her travels had always fascinated him.

"I was in a garden there." She leaned back on her heels, her gaze on some far distant place. "There were the most massive tomatoes and I was picking the best." She stopped and grinned at him. "To make sauce for lasagna. Or rather, Mamma Francesca was teaching me how to make it. Those tomatoes were so delicious."

"Cool," he murmured, watching the wash

of sun light up her face. Gemma was gorgeous. Then shadows filled her eyes.

"I don't know what else happened," she murmured. "I can't—"

"Remember," he finished for her and winked.

"Exactly!" Gemma exclaimed. She burst out laughing and the tense lines dissipated.

They worked together for a while in a genial silence that required no speaking. Jake had a hunch she was remembering more, but he remained quiet, loathe to interrupt.

"I must have been to Italy several times," she eventually murmured. "In my mind I can see the Coliseum, the tower of Pisa and a spot on a mountain where there was an eruption."

"Vesuvius," Jake offered.

"No. Mt. Etna. Three days after Kurt and I left, there was an eruption. It was a big tour group and we were so glad we hadn't delayed..." Gemma blinked several times, then twisted her head to look at him. "Why can't I remember my husband, Jake?"

"You will. But you have a lot of memories tucked in that lovely head. I guess they can't all come at once." He kept working.

"What am I supposed to do until I do remember?" A hint of bitterness colored her voice. "That's part of what bothers me with the whole Alexa thing. What do I have to offer her? I don't remember how to lead a tour anymore, but even if I did, how could I travel *and* care for a child? Or am I supposed to stay here and freeload off the aunts until I remember my life? If I ever do, that is."

"Gemma," Jake scolded. "Last year your sister was injured while rock climbing. Nobody thought she was freeloading when she stayed in bed to let her leg heal. Olivia happily took over her job."

"Victoria always did love scaling the most treacherous places," Gemma muttered, apparently unaware that she'd identified which sister without any prompting. "But this is different. I don't work here."

"Maybe you could for a while," he suggested.

"Doing what?" she asked, eyebrows arched. "Showing people around? Kind of hard since I don't know my own way around the place."

"You'll figure it out. Give it some thought. I'm sure you'll find a niche in The Haven's ministry that only you can fill." He paused before asking, "What will you do about Alexa?"

Gemma rose. She studied the group of kids playing dodgeball nearby in a grassy meadow. Then she considered the circle of stones they'd gathered around last evening to roast marshmallows. Lastly she surveyed the play equipment her sisters used for their own children. She remained silent for some time. When she did speak there was a hesitancy to her words that told Jake she was struggling to sort out her emotions.

"I think I'll ask Victoria to find out if Alexa can come here for a visit."

"That's a great idea." Jake hoped she wouldn't change her mind. A lonely child could be exactly what Gemma needed to take her mind off her own problems.

"We can get to know each other. I don't want to abandon this child whom my husband apparently cared for so deeply," she murmured, forehead pleated. "But what if—?"

"I'll help you," he interrupted, wondering why he was doing this when he'd spent the past six years basically isolating himself at The Haven. Now he was going to help with some orphaned little girl he didn't even know? *Yes.*

"Thank you, Jake." Gemma's smile somehow made it all make sense. "What will we do with her?"

"Help her join in the activities with all the other kids," he said, glancing over her head at a group of kids now flying kites. "There's always something to do here."

"I suppose." The way Gemma dragged out the word proved he'd missed the intent of her question. "I actually meant what will *I* do with her? What kind of things would help me get to know Alexa?"

"You were always good with kids, Gem. You'll think of something. And you do have Kurt in common. But I'm not sure you need to plan it all out ahead of time," he cautioned. "Maybe you wait, watch to see what she enjoys and build on that."

"How did you get to be so smart about kids, Jake?" Gemma moved farther down the row, annihilating weeds as if driven.

"I'm not smart about kids," he denied as the familiar surge of loss bloomed inside. *I didn't get that chance. Don't go there.* "Hey," he challenged, desperate to change the subject. "Are you doing the corn rows or am I?"

"You take forever. I'll do it." She shot him a cheeky grin. "You always baby the seedlings

too much. Once they're out of your greenhouse and in the ground, they'll toughen up.
You have to be strong to live in the foothills
of the Rockies."

"So now *you're* the gardener who's giving
me advice?" He relaxed, comfortable with
their familiar banter. "Any suggestions you
want to share about the rhubarb? Your aunts
want three more plants."

"What on earth for?" Gemma's nose wrinkled with distaste. "It's so sour."

"Not when Adele mixes it with my strawberries and adds a big dollop of ice cream.
What?" he demanded when she hooted with
laughter.

"You can't grow strawberries here, Jake."
She looked so alive, so vibrant, so... Gemma.

He'd forgotten she hadn't visited last summer because she'd been escorting a group on
a cruise through the Northwest Passage. So
now, of course, she razed him mercilessly
about trying to grow delicate strawberry
plants at this elevation. Jake endured it for

a little while, but with his pride at stake, he finally rose and beckoned.

"Follow me, oh doubting one," he ordered.

Gemma had always been lousy at hiding her emotions and right now her curiosity was in control. She dusted off her grubby gloves against her dirty knees and hopped across the rows to follow him.

"Where are we going?"

"Wait for it." He led her around an outcropping of stones. "Feast your eyes on my strawberry garden, doubter." He drew one fat red fruit off its stem and ensured it was relatively clean before setting it on her palm. "First berry of the season."

Wide-eyed, Gemma inspected the fruit before popping it into her mouth. A flush of satisfaction filled Jake when she slowed her chewing to allow the flavors to permeate her taste buds. Her zest for life, her eagerness about everything it offered, that's what he wanted her to recover.

"Well?" he demanded, stupidly eager to hear her opinion.

"Amazing." Her big expansive smile did funny things to his stomach. "How did you get them to survive?"

Jake figured his explanation probably went into too much detail and droned on for too long, but Gemma seemed to listen to every word. This was the old Gem. This intense interest in life was what had first drawn him to her.

"So by packing those stones around to soak in the heat, and by raising the beds, you create a warmer, sheltered area." She clapped her hands together. "Bravo, Monsieur Horticulturalist."

He'd missed her enthusiasm.

"Yield?" She bent to study the way he'd laid the new runners.

"Last year was good. It's too early to tell this year." Funny how pleased he was by her interest. "I'm hopeful we'll get enough for Adele to freeze for next…"

Suddenly Gemma wasn't listening. She gazed over the valley, but Jake doubted she was seeing the meadow with its wildflowers waving in the wind. Something else was going on inside that auburn head.

"Why do I keep thinking about roses, Jake?" She turned to frown at him, green eyes dark and swirling. "Is it something to do with my past?"

He shook his head.

"Mine," he said very quietly. Of all things, why did she have to remember that?

Eyes stretched wide, she waited for an explanation.

"I grow roses in the greenhouse." He pushed past a tide of memories. "I experiment with them."

"The Lilian." Her frown deepened. "I keep hearing that name."

"We should finish up weeding. It will soon be time for dinner." He wanted to walk away, to ignore her question, to retreat to the silence that he should never have left.

Jake wanted to leave, but he couldn't ignore Gem's question, not when she was so desperate to learn about her past. Besides, The Lilian was part of her past, too.

"I'm sorry if I said something wrong." Her hand touched his fleetingly. "I didn't mean to."

"It's okay. The Lilian was a prototype of a rose that I used to work on when you lived here before. In memory of—someone," he substituted at the last moment.

"Which has to do with the funeral you mentioned, doesn't it? I'm sorry." Gemma said it so quickly that Jake figured he must have visibly reacted. "We don't need to talk about it."

She walked to the corn rows and began industriously weeding between stalks. Jake watched her for a few minutes, but he couldn't stay. Mention of The Lilian had brought back his old restlessness along with a wealth of excruciatingly painful memories. He had to get out of here before they overwhelmed him and turned him into a weeping wimp.

Take them tomorrow, Jake. Don't go today, please? What does one more day matter?

Lily's voice.

Teeth gritted, he wheeled around and strode out of the garden enclosure, carefully latching the gate to keep out invaders before he race-walked to his small cabin. Inside he made himself a thermos of strong coffee, grabbed a couple of protein bars and changed into his hiking boots. Backpack secure and walking stick in hand, he stepped onto the trail he hiked whenever he needed to break free of his past.

When Jake reached the top of the first incline, he ignored the voice in his head and turned back. Gemma was still in the garden, but now she stood, one hand shading her eyes as she looked directly at him, motionless for several moments. Then she knelt and continued with her weeding, as if she understood that he wanted to be alone.

Wanted to be alone? No.

But that's the way it was. Would always be. *Had* to be.

Gemma set the foil-covered dishes on the counter in Jake's cabin and moved toward the door. She didn't want to look around, didn't want to invade his personal space when he wasn't there. But she couldn't help noticing how clean, how sterile everything seemed.

No pictures of loved ones. No books on side tables. Nothing left lying around. Nothing to hint at the intriguing man who'd abandoned her in the garden earlier and hadn't yet returned.

Her fingers were reaching for the door handle when it opened.

"Hi." Jake stood there, studying her.

"Hi. You missed dinner, so the aunts sent me over with some," she blurted, feeling the heat singe her cheeks. "I didn't mean to intrude."

"You're not. But you shouldn't have gone to the trouble. I'm not very hungry." He stepped inside, set his pack on the tiny table and faced her. "Thank you though."

"It's Adele's lasagna and it's amazing." She blinked, then grinned. "You probably already know that. See you."

Gemma scurried back to the house, feeling like a frightened rabbit. The barrenness of Jake's quarters and his earlier reticence after she'd asked about The Lillian frightened her. Was that because subconsciously she knew that if he answered all her questions, if he was completely honest with her, she'd know for sure that she didn't belong at The Haven?

But if she didn't belong here, then where did she belong? Certainly not in the cheap Toronto apartment the aunts had described. Not anymore. From their description she'd figured it was a tiny place where newlyweds constantly ran into each other and enjoyed it. That romantic place belonged to another newly married Gemma.

This Gemma didn't want to go there, didn't want to feel even more out of place, even more distanced from the woman whom everyone but she remembered. More than that, she didn't want to *not* belong anywhere else. So during dinner she'd asked her aunts how she could have her things moved without physically traveling to Toronto. Of course they had a friend who had a friend and by next week everything she and Kurt owned would supposedly arrive here at The Haven. And then what?

Her mind immediately turned to Jake. He'd help her deal with it. She didn't know why she was so sure of that, she just knew it was true. But was it fair to ask him?

Gemma had so many questions about her rescuer and very few answers. So far Jake was the only one who'd expressly said she belonged here.

If only she could believe him.

Chapter Four

"Relax, Gem. You're going to love Alexa."

Jake hoped he sounded confident because he'd grown as nervous as Gemma while they waited for the arrival of a new group of foster children looking forward to a weekend of fun at The Haven. Alexa was traveling with them.

"You don't know that. But anyway, here they come." Gemma patted her ponytail as if there could be any improvement on that reddish-gold swath of glistening waves. "I hope—"

She didn't finish that sentence, but her longing was visible to Jake. That's how well he knew her. He knew she wanted a fresh start, to make a connection with someone who knew as little about her as she did them, someone who had no preconceptions about her. Someone she didn't have to remember.

When Gem's hand slid into his, Jake startled. She must have felt that because she glanced at him.

"Do you mind?"

Mind? How could he? Holding her hand, helping her however he could, made him feel ten feet tall. It also worried him. He was hoping she'd take a keen interest in Alexa, and not only for the child's sake. But he needed to make sure he didn't get too involved with Gemma.

"Hang on to me whenever you want," he said in a breezy tone.

Gemma frowned at him in that discerning way that said she suspected his genuineness.

"I mean it. Oh, oh. Those three boys look tough, don't they?" Jake spoke mostly to calm Gemma. "Those four girls are just as tough looking. But where's—ah." His breath escaped in a rush as the last passenger, a boy of perhaps twelve, helped a young girl down the steps. "That must be Alexa."

"Really?" Gem pulled the small picture from her pocket and studied it. "I guess. Someone cut her beautiful hair. Badly."

The boy said something to Alexa who nodded and remained in place. He hurried toward Victoria who was directing children toward their counsellors. Alexa clung to a ragged doll as she peered around curiously. The other kids had obviously visited The Haven before and knew the routine. Alexa kept scanning the area. Jake knew the exact moment she recognized Gemma because she began walking toward them.

"You're Gemma," she said, stopping in front of them.

"Yes, I am." Gemma blinked her surprise. "How did you know?"

"Kurt tol' me all 'bout you an' he gave me a picture. Is he here? I want to see him. I didn't see him for a long time 'cause he was workin'." Alexa scanned the area hopefully.

"I, uh." Gemma gulped and glanced at Jake. All he could do was nod for her to continue. "He isn't here, sweetheart. He had to go away and—"

"Like Mommy had to go 'way?" Tears pooled in Alexa's big blue eyes at Gemma's nod. "The lady tole me Mommy's never coming back. Isn't Kurt c-comin' back neither?"

Her obvious pain touched Jake's soul. Poor little orphan girl.

"I'm so sorry, Alexa, but Kurt died," Gemma said very gently. "He wanted to see you, but there was an accident and—"

"A acc'dent. Jus' like Mommy." Alexa's sad sigh of resignation brought tears to Jake's eyes. Such a tiny child to have experienced so much grief in her short life.

"Everybody's gone away, 'cept me. I don't like bein' alone," she said to Gemma, her voice wobbling as if she was ready to burst into tears.

"I know exactly how you feel, Alexa." Gemma beckoned the little girl to join her in sitting on a rock. "I feel like I'm all alone, too."

"Why? You gots this big house an' this man here an' everythin'." Alexa managed a watery smile for Jake. "I'm Alexa."

"Nice to meet you," he said with a chuckle. "I'm Jake."

"Hi, Jake." She held out her tiny hand to shake his and then returned to the subject. "This is where you an' Kurt live?"

"No, we never lived here together. We lived in a big city, but I can't remember that." Strain etched spider lines at the corners of Gemma's green eyes. "I can't remember Kurt or The Haven or Jake either. A rock hit me," she explained before the child could ask.

"An' that made you not remember nothin'?" Alexa's blue eyes grew huge.

"Mostly nothing." She nodded. "So I'm all alone, too, Alexa. Maybe we could be friends?"

Jake didn't like hearing Gemma say she was all alone, and yet her words had emerged without thought, as if that was how she really felt. He'd have to think about changing her perceptions without letting their relationship develop too deeply. It wouldn't be easy, but he'd done it before. He could do it again. Couldn't he?

"You're too big to be my friend." Alexa giggled. "My friends are s'posed to be little like me."

"Well, Kurt was your friend and he wasn't little." Gemma raised her eyebrows at Alexa as if to ask what she thought of that.

"Yeah. 'Kay." Alexa shrugged before looking around. "Arthur tol' me we're gonna have juice and cookies. I want some."

"Arthur is...?" Gemma waited while Alexa explained about the boy who had stayed with her for the entire ride.

"He's over there by that lady. Arthur din't wanna come here," Alexa murmured after she'd waved at him and yelled that she was okay. "He likes hockey better. C'n he play hockey here?"

"If it was wintertime our creek would be frozen and we'd have a party skating on it. But it's almost summer now so the ice is all melted. It's still lots of fun though." Apparently unaware that she'd revealed knowledge of her past, Gemma rose and held out her hand. "I can see Arthur's going inside. Let's go join him, Alexa. Coming, Jake?"

"I guess I've got time for a quick break, though by the looks of that bed, I should do some more flower planting." Jake walked with them toward The Haven's kitchen because he wanted to watch their interaction a little longer.

"C'n I help you plant? I love flowers," Alexa asked enthusiastically.

"Sure. But maybe not today," he said. "I've got something else I need to do first."

"What're ya gonna do?" Alexa studied him.

"I think I know." Gemma's snicker told him she understood his dour expression. "My aunts just bought a new cow. Her name is Sweetie, but I think Jake calls her something else, something not nice."

"Why? Is she a bad cow?" Alexa wondered, grabbing both their hands and skipping between them. "Maybe she don't like it here. Maybe she don't got no friends here neither."

"Maybe she won't make any if she keeps swatting me with that tail of hers," he mumbled and then realized they'd both heard him. "Sweetie—terrible name by the way—and I have some discussing to do."

"You c'n talk to a cow?" The child's big blue eyes gaped at him. "C'n you teach *me* cow talk?"

Gemma burst into laughter and Jake had to join her. This child was going to be good for Gemma. Maybe for him, too?

"First, snack time. Then we'll see," he said,

noting Gemma's big smile. "Perhaps by then you'll remember how to clean the barn."

"Ew! I don't want to remember that!" With a toss of her auburn ponytail, Gemma grasped the little girl's hand and led her inside. "Come on, Alexa. I'm told Friday's doughnut day at The Haven. I snuck one and they're scrumptious."

"Did Kurt like 'em?"

Gemma paused. Her gaze flew to Jake, a question in the depths. Then she took a deep breath and hunkered down to Alexa's level.

"How could he not?" she murmured, her face troubled as she traced one hand over the badly shorn strands of shiny blond hair.

"I can tell you Kurt loved doughnuts." Jake spoke past the lump in his throat. "And Gemma. And you, Alexa. He was a very smart man." Satisfied that both females were now smiling, he said, "Let's eat, ladies."

Gemma spent all afternoon with Alexa, shocked by the comfort she found in the child's company, even though the little girl had boundless energy and just as many questions—about everything.

"Is Jake your boyfriend?" she asked as they planted some flower seeds in pots.

"What? No. I hardly know him." Flustered, Gemma tried to interest the little girl in watching birds. "Besides, I was married. To Kurt, remember?"

"Jake likes you," Alexa insisted.

"How can you tell?" Curious to hear the child's response, she sank onto the grass and watched the little girl stab seeds into the soil.

"'Cause he got you a big glass of iced tea an' the best chair an' the doughnut with the mostest icing on it." Alexa nodded wisely. "That means he likes you."

"Jake's nice," Gemma agreed, hoping they could leave it at that, because she didn't want to examine her friendship with Jake too closely. Not yet.

Finished seeding, they wandered around The Haven until Jake showed up with a couple of fishing rods and cajoled them down to the river. At first Gemma protested that she didn't want to fish, but she gave in when Jake insisted. With the sun waning over the western mountains, she found a certain calm in sitting on a rock and casting her line into the bubbling water. That tranquility quickly dissipated when a fish jerked her line.

"Why choose mine?" she mumbled, feeling stupid and inept.

"'Cause it's tryin' to be your friend. Turn the thingamajig," Alexa advised, almost bouncing on her toes as she watched the fish flip in and out of the water, ignoring her own rod, which was in danger of falling into the creek.

"Jake!" Gemma desperately wished she'd chosen to read a book this afternoon.

"Stop yelling. You'll scare away all the fish and I haven't caught any yet," he grumbled from behind her left shoulder, his voice reassuring. "Slowly reel the line in. You've done it a hundred times before, Gem."

"Maybe, but I don't remember that." And then, all at once she knew exactly what to do. She slowly turned the handle on the reel, judging the distance. When the fish jerked, she gave it some line then resumed winding. Finally, without even realizing her intent, she leaned over and drew it from the water just before the fish could take off again. "Okay. Now what?"

"Now we put it in our bucket." Jake calmly disentangled the hook and plopped the fish into the pail of water. "We'll clean them later. That's your job, by the way."

Clean fish? Gemma couldn't dredge up a single memory of doing that.

"Doesn't The Haven practice catch and release?" she asked desperately.

"Not when it's my dinner." Jake grinned. "You can cast again now."

"Uh-huh." With him watching her so closely, Gemma had to do something. She deliberately miscast and landed her hook in the rocks. "Oh, dear."

Jake's smirk and the shake of his head told her he knew she was avoiding catching more.

"Mine's stuck," Alexa muttered. "I can't—oof!" She jerked the rod so hard, it pulled the line out. A flapping fish passed over their heads to land on a rock behind them. "I caught a fish," she said, dumbfounded.

"You sure did, although your technique needs a little refining. Let's take a picture." He pulled out his phone and snapped a shot of Alexa holding her fish. "Good work, kiddo. Now, let's put it in the bucket."

"Hey, mine's the biggest," Alexa pronounced. "Can I try again?"

"Sure." Jake reset her line, offered encouragement when her first few casts had no results and then resumed his own fishing. "She's a great kid, Gem," he murmured. "No wonder Kurt loved her."

"You're really good with her." Gemma hadn't thought of Jake as the fatherly type, but somehow it seemed right.

"You didn't expect me to be good with kids when I work at The Haven where there are kids around all the time?" He chuckled. "No-brainer."

"You should have your own kids, Jake," she said, thinking how lucky that child would be.

"I did once." Barely audible, the words seemed squeezed out of him. Immediately his lips pursed as if to stop any further revelations.

"Where are they now?" Gemma regretted asking when his whole body froze.

"*He* died." Cold, stark, void of emotion.

"The funeral you spoke of. It was your son's." She reached out and touched his arm. "I'm so sorry, Jake."

"Thanks." He withdrew his arm on the pretext of helping Alexa who was happily reeling in her second fish.

Gemma pretended to concentrate on her own rod while she tried to make sense of what she'd learned. Jake was a dad who'd lost his son. How? Where was his wife? Did her aunts and her sisters know about his past? Had she known? Questions abounded, but his closed expression deterred her from asking.

She shivered, suddenly chilly though the temperature hadn't changed. Jake and Alexa caught more fish while Gemma let her hook dangle in the shallow water as her tired brain tried to put the pieces of Jake's past together.

"We've a good catch of fish." His voice drew her out of her reverie. "Time to clean them now. Then we'll cook them up."

"I think Adele's cooking ribs for dinner," Gemma murmured.

"That's good because I was thinking we could share these with a friend of mine. He lives in town." Jake smiled at Alexa. "Would you like to have a fish dinner with my friend?"

"Is Gem comin'?" Alexa glanced her way anxiously, obviously relieved when she nodded.

"Maybe I am. Who's your friend?" Gemma asked.

"Billy Hooper." Jake grinned at her gasp.

"He's still alive? He must be nearly a hundred now." Gemma blinked. How did she know that when she couldn't even conjure up Billy's face?

"Ninety-seven. And you know how he loves fish dinners." Jake stored their hooks and bundled the rods into their leather bag. From it he extracted a filleting knife and a honing stone, which he used to sharpen the knife. "See that big, flat stone over there?" he said to Alexa. She nodded. "That's where we'll clean the fish. Then we can leave what we don't want for the birds to eat."

"'Cause they get hungry, too, right?" Alexa seemed not at all squeamish as Jake slit open the fish.

For some reason Gemma caught herself paying close attention to how he achieved the first fillet. While he slipped it into a plastic bag, she found herself rising.

"I'll do it." She stared at him and gulped. Where had that come from?

"You're sure?" Jake inspected her, a twinkle glimmering in his eyes.

"Actually, no," she admitted, her mouth dry. "It just seems like… I should fillet," she told him after a moment's pause.

"You should," he agreed with a smile and handed her the knife. "You're much better at it than I am. Another gift you've remembered. Let's see if your hands remember the skill."

Gemma stepped in front of the rock. She considered the fish he'd laid there. Blankness filled her brain.

"I don't know—" And then suddenly she did know. Almost of their own accord, her fingers slid the knife under the slippery scales, automatically freeing perfectly smooth, thin filets. When the fish was deboned she looked at Jake and grinned. "Who knew?"

"You did." He laughed at her smug smile. "You've got a ton of other talents, Gem. You just need to let them out."

When all the fish were in the bag, they washed the knife and pail and their hands in the creek water. Jake dumped the fish remains on a pile of stones downstream. No sooner had they moved a few feet away than gulls, eagles and ravens homed in on the food.

"They like it!" Alexa exclaimed, clapping her hands. "Don't fight," she yelled and waved her arms for emphasis. "Hey." She frowned at Jake. "They're goin'. Did I scare 'em?"

"No. It's spring, so they're taking the food to feed their babies. There won't be a scrap left." His face as he gazed at the little girl made Gemma's stomach clench. How gentle and kind he was. Perfect for working with kids at The Haven. He clearly belonged here.

But where did she belong?

"Can we stop by the house before we go to Billy's?" Jake asked.

"We don't need to," Gemma began before noticing his expression. "But we can. Why?"

"Billy doesn't eat that well. I usually take along extra food for his lunch tomorrow. Adele will have it ready." He waited for them to precede him up the hill. At the top Gemma agreed that Alexa could skip ahead.

"How did you get so involved with Billy?" she asked.

"I work with a church group who help seniors who want to stay in their homes but need a little support to do it." He shrugged. "Fix a roof, empty eavestroughs, find someone to clean or do laundry, organize meals or shopping, visit and share a meal. Simple stuff like that."

"But isn't there a women's group…" Gemma paused as a memory flickered to life. "Never mind. I doubt Billy would tolerate a female in his home."

"I told you it would all come back to you." Jake grinned at her. "There are several senior men like Billy in our little community who are quite capable of living alone but have other needs. Sometimes all they really need is coffee time with another male and some good, strong man-stuff discussions."

"Man stuff?" she teased, one eyebrow lifted.

"Just sayin'. Billy grew up almost a century ago when it was different for men and women. Besides, there's Ethel." His nose wrinkled.

"Ethel Denman?" She saw Jake nod and frowned. "Why, she must be as old as him. They should have lots in common."

"Not so much. Ethel's mostly interested in husband hunting Billy. He is *not* interested in that, even though she keeps baking her special prune-and-bran custard pie for him."

"Prune and bran pie?" Gemma gaped at him in disbelief. He wore such a comical expression she burst out laughing. "No wonder he's not interested. It sounds awful. So you really are a white knight."

"Me? No, just not well equipped for other services in the church. I tried ushering but I dropped the offering plate. Can you say *fired*?" He grimaced comically, but she knew he was minimizing his abilities. "I want to be involved and this allows me to help yet still have some flexibility. Hopefully I don't mess up too badly."

"So that's the reason for all those phone calls on the drive here. I think it's wonderful. You must be kept very busy." She called to Alexa who was petting her aunts' rescue dogs, Spot and Dot. "We're going to visit someone so we should wash up first, kiddo."

"'Kay." The biddable child followed Gemma inside. She asked such a plethora of questions that Gemma was glad when they returned to find Jake waiting by his truck.

"She doesn't take *I don't remember* for an answer," she whispered after he'd fastened the car seat he'd borrowed for Alexa.

"Neither did you once," he reminded. "You two are a matched set."

Gemma thought about that as Jake drove to Billy's. Had she been like Alexa? It was so frustrating trying to remember when her stupid brain only recalled dumb stuff like filleting fish.

"You're doing fine, Gem. Don't force it. It will—oh, boy." Jake parked quickly and jumped out of the truck to intervene between a red-faced Billy Hooper who was thumping his cane on the doorstep, apparently trying to silence Ethel Denman who was pretending to wash windows while trying to peer inside Billy's home.

"Come on, Alexa," she said, unfastening her seat belt and doing the same for the child. "It seems we're going to be peacemakers for a while."

"What's a peacemaker?"

Gemma rolled her eyes at the nine-hundredth question before stepping forward to greet the elderly woman and divert her attention. She thought she heard Jake mutter thank you, but since he kept his expression totally blasé it was hard to tell.

"I'm stuck," Ethel said with a glare at Billy.

"This garden is a mess, like everything else around here."

"Then why do you keep coming here?" he demanded in a growly tone.

Gemma helped Jake ease Ethel's skirt off the long rose thorns that had trapped her.

"Isn't this fun, Gem?" Jake muttered.

Oddly enough, with Jake it really *was*.

Chapter Five

"You gots a really dirty house, Mr. Billy," Alexa said bluntly after her first step over the threshold. "We gotta clean it."

Wonder of wonders, after choking back his surprise, Billy agreed. He also agreed that Alexa and Gemma could dust, but only *if* Jake made their entire dinner. So now Jake was at the stove.

"Billy, if you keep forbidding Ethel entry, she'll only grow more eager to get inside," he argued as he fried their catch of fish. Gemma's snicker was low but he still heard it.

"As if anything could stop that determined woman," she muttered.

Jake didn't disagree. But the place was a disaster and he figured Billy had agreed to let the females dust only because he thought it was a woman's place to do so and because Ethel had threatened to call the health department. Thank the Lord Gemma hadn't minded pitching in, though now she was swiping her cloth across the fireplace mantle with a disgusted look that said she figured Ethel's idea was spot-on.

"Nobody fries fish like you do, Jakey." While everyone else labored, Billy happily lounged in his tattered recliner.

"Jakey?" A wicked grin played with the corners of Gemma's mouth. She turned her back, but her shaking shoulders told Jake she was enjoying his embarrassment.

Jakey ignored her to concentrate on his cooking. He had everything ready just as Gemma and Alexa pronounced the main area dusted, though not, he noted, dust-free. Still, it was a first step. When everyone was seated around Billy's heavy oak table, Alexa insisted on holding hands before they said grace. Jake liked the feel of Gemma's soft fingers curling around his as the old man offered a fulsome prayer of thanks for the food. Then they ate.

"Ooh, this is so good. I can remember when last I..." Gemma shook her head once. "It's very good, Jake."

"I never had this kinda dinner afore," Alexa told him. "An' I never caught no fish neither." She studied Billy for a moment before asserting, "You should'a comed fishin' with us. Gem's good at—" she turned to Gemma "—whad'ya call it again?"

"Filleting," Gemma responded. She held out Billy's tiny antique glass pitcher and suggested, "Try a bit of this vinegar on your fish. It's delish."

"That rhymes." Alexa's giggle made everyone smile.

After dinner Gemma insisted Jake and Billy sit outside with their coffee while she and Alexa cleaned up. Seeing the glint in her eyes, Jake knew better than to refuse. If he knew Gemma, she intended to load that seldom-used dishwasher to the brim. While it ran, he figured she'd coax Alexa to help her turn the dingy kitchen into a gleaming space. It was like old times. Gemma fit in wherever she went and managed to help someone along the way. Jake liked that. A lot.

Outside, when Billy plied him with questions about her, Jake told him about the earthquake.

"So when's she going to be normal again?"

"Gem's normal now, Billy. She just can't remember some stuff." Some people might have taken Billy's aggressive questions the wrong way, but Jake had known him long enough to recognize the glint of concern lurking in the back of the old fellow's amber gaze. "Doctors say her memory will return when her brain's ready. Nothing to do but wait."

"What's she going to do till then?" Billy

demanded. "Doing nothing while staying with those two old ladies will drive her bonkers. Least it would me."

To Billy other seniors were old. The description did not apply to himself.

"I'm not sure," he said quietly.

"She sure is a good-looking girl, Jakey. You interested?"

The meddling old codger! Half amused, half irritated, Jake shook his head. "No."

"Why not? She's sure as shooting pretty. Bible says a man ought not to be alone," Billy quoted.

"You're alone, Billy," Jake pointed out. He almost groaned as he realized Gemma could probably hear every matchmaking word through the open kitchen window.

"That's different. Ain't nobody can replace my Irma." Billy's chin thrust out.

"No reason you have to replace her, but a little companionship would be good for you." Stubbornness set the old guy's face into rigid lines. "Besides, you've forgotten something," Jake mused, tongue in cheek. "Those ladies who'd like to come calling on you are fantastic bakers. Seems dumb not to take advantage of that."

It wasn't just that Billy didn't eat well. Jake also worried his friend was alone too often. Using the pretense of food, visitors could keep him interested in community life and thereby divert a lapse into loneliness and depression that often overtook solitary seniors. If Billy would let them in.

"Bakers, huh? Never thought of it that way. Now that the place is cleaned up some—" A cunning grin flashed across his weathered face. "Maybe I'll let that know-it-all Ethel come calling if she brings me a pie. An' I don't mean that prune thing."

Jake shook his head. No sense remonstrating with the man. Billy had his own way of doing things. At least he'd agreed to allow a visitor. That was progress.

His serenity was shattered a moment later by Alexa's raised voice.

"C'n I stay at The Haven all the time?"

"You mean permanently?" Gemma sounded shocked. "I—who would look after you?"

"I don't need nobody. That dumb ol' Kurt tol' me I was a big girl an' could look after my mom an' me." Belligerence laced the girl's voice.

"Are you mad at Kurt, sweetheart?" Gemma asked in a very soft voice.

"Yeah." Alexa's sobs came through the window clearly.

"He didn't leave you on purpose, Alexa. He couldn't help that there was an earth-quake and he died. He didn't *want* to go away." Gemma's certainty made Jake think of Lily. She hadn't wanted—

"Those old aunties said Kurt's in a bet-ter place now." Alexa sniffed. "They musta been talkin' 'bout heaven 'cause that's what people said when my mom died, but I don't think it's better."

Jake figured memory or not, Gemma was

hunkered down in front of the little girl, ready to listen and, if possible, help her. That was Gemma. Heart of gold.

"Why isn't it better?" she asked in a soothing voice.

"'Cause I'm not with her!" Alexa wailed. Then a pause. "D'you think Kurt an' my mom *like* not havin' me with them?" she demanded incredulously. Her sad sniff said her little heart was breaking at the thought.

"That's not what the aunties meant. Of course Kurt and your mommy would like to be with you, but they are also glad to be with God. Where they are, there is no pain, no sadness, no wishing things would be better. Where they are is wonderful. I don't think they'd want you there though, at least not right now."

"Why not?" Alexa demanded. Jake visualized her tiny fists planted on her hips.

"Because it's not your time to be there," Gemma said quietly. "The Bible says there's a time for everything. A time like now for leaves to grow and seeds to grow. And then there's a time for the leaves to turn color and fall off."

"An' then it's time for snow," Alexa chirped happily.

"Yes. There's a season for everything," Gemma said. "Right now is our season of missing Kurt and you missing your mom. You want it to be like it was before, but it can't be. I know it's hard to understand, honey, but I believe God wants you to stay right here on earth."

"Why?" The barrage of kid-questions made Jake grin.

"I can't tell you why. You'd have to ask Him to tell you that. I will tell you what I believe." Jake could hear the smile lacing Gemma's voice. "I think here is where you belong, at least right now. You helped me get through the awful time today when I couldn't remember filleting and you cheered me up. I think that for now you belong at The Haven, Alexa."

That sounded exactly like the old Gemma. He could hear her voice from the past. *God knows what He's doing. Get with His program.*

"Where do you belong, Gemma?" the little voice squeaked.

A long silence followed. Jake tensed. Then Gemma murmured, "I don't know. Yet."

As they drove back to The Haven, Alexa nodded off. That was okay because Gemma's head whirled with the day's events. She was going to talk to Jake about it when a call came through his dash screen.

"Hey, Olivia. How's it going?"

"I'm in a pickle, Jake, and hoping you can do me a favor." Gemma frowned at Olivia's harried tone.

"Name it." Jake pulled to the side of the road and set his flashers going so he could fully listen to her request.

"A friend took Eli to soccer practice. I'm supposed to be there in half an hour to pick him up because Gabe's with a trail-riding group from The Haven. But the baby's really fussing and won't settle and—"

"Say no more. We'll go watch Eli practice and then bring him home," Jake quickly offered.

"Who's we?" Olivia wanted to know.

"Gemma, Alexa—who is Kurt's stepdaughter—and me," he explained. "We just came from sharing our fish dinner with Billy Hooper."

"Hey, Gem. So you're back fishing. Your most favorite activity. How's Alexa?" Olivia asked.

"Sleeping right now. But she's fine. Who's Eli?" Gemma asked and then felt silly for not knowing. "I don't think I met him."

"Eli was away on a school field trip the day you came home. He's Gabe's son from his first marriage. He's a great kid—" Olivia paused midsentence before saying hurriedly, "That's Mirella again. I have to go. Thank you so much, you two. I appreciate it."

"Our pleasure, Livvie. See you later." Jake pushed the off button. Then he glanced at Gemma. "You don't mind, do you?"

"Of course not. I'd like to meet Eli. Besides, you *are* the local fixer," she teased. "This is just another wrinkle for you to smooth."

Jake shot her a droll look before turning around and heading back to town.

"Do you think my sister is happy with her life?" she asked.

"Very." Jake needed no deliberation over that. "I think all four of you found happiness in your marriages."

"Did you?" The question slipped out before Gemma could think about it. Given the grim look on Jake's face, it was obvious the subject was painful. "Sorry, I—"

"I was very happy," Jake muttered. Then he clamped his lips together so tightly Gemma knew not to ask more. They drove through town. He pulled into a parking spot by the soccer field where the players were already going through their drills. "That's Eli," he said, pointing. He waved at the gangly boy.

"Good-looking kid," Gemma said, hoping to break the tenseness between them. "Wake up, Alexa."

Once she'd explained what they were doing and Jake had told Eli they'd take him home when he was finished practice, they found seats in the bleachers and watched the players. Most of the parents seemed to be coaching which meant that after a few greetings they were virtually alone in the stands. When a bored Alexa asked to join three children kicking a ball behind them, Gemma agreed. Jake remained silent.

"I wasn't trying to pry," she apologized when it seemed he'd never talk to her again. "It just kind of slipped out. I'm sorry. I shouldn't ask so many questions."

He stared at her for several moments, his blue eyes stormy. She didn't look away. Finally he sighed.

"Look, if I tell you, can we let it go? It is not something I want to rehash ever again."

Gemma nodded, afraid to speak lest he change his mind.

"I was married and we had a baby son. I was starting a new business, a greenhouse business, and I was in debt up to my neck—past it. I had a contract to deliver a truckload of my best poinsettias three weeks before Christmas." He closed his eyes. His low voice grew forced, as if each word took an enormous amount of courage. "The plants took a ton of time and effort, but they were gorgeous and at their peak. I had to deliver them on time because fulfilling that contract meant we'd have enough cash for my bedding-plant season, and it meant I could concentrate on my specialty."

"Roses." Gemma wondered how she knew that.

"Yes." Jake gave her a sidelong glance. It was several moments before he spoke again. "I was totally focused on getting the poinsettias to market at the promised time. No way could I return the deposit I'd been given. We'd already spent most of it on new stock and house renovations. I felt I had to show up as contracted."

"Okay." What was so terrible about that? But as she waited, Gemma's misgivings grew. "You don't have to tell—"

"I delivered the plants with no problem. But on my return I got caught in a freak ice storm. I slipped off the icy road and had to spend the night in my truck with no cell coverage to call home. It was a deserted road so no rescuers." His voice sounded edgy. "Lily hadn't wanted me to leave. She was ill and the baby had a cold. She begged me to put it off one more day, but I was so sure I could make the run and get home with no problem." His face hardened. "Instead I got stuck in the ditch, helpless until the storm spent itself. In the morning, help finally came, but it was too late."

His voice had dropped and his face

had hardened into a white strained mask. Gemma knew that whatever was coming wasn't good.

"When I got home I found Lily and Thomas dead from carbon monoxide poisoning from the fireplace, which I'd loaded up before I left."

"Oh, Jake." She touched his arm, her heart aching for his devastating loss. "I'm so sorry."

"I killed them, Gem." His eyes, now hardened chips of Arctic ice, glared at her. "It was my fault they died. Lily had been complaining for ages about the fireplace not being right. I kept promising her I'd fix it. That day I'd even told her I'd do it when I got home." His eyes looked dead. "I put my wife and child's safety second and business first. What kind of husband—father—does that, Gem?"

She wanted to tell him it wasn't his fault, but Jake suddenly lurched to his feet and stalked away. When Alexa would have followed him, Gemma called her back, sensing that the handyman needed privacy.

"Jake's thinking about something, honey. Let's leave him alone for a while, okay?" Relieved when the child nodded and returned to her playmates, Gemma visually tracked the handyman until he disappeared from sight. "Oh, Lord, please. His burden is so great. Help me know what to do to help him."

She didn't know where the words came from, had no idea if her prayer was even appropriate. She only knew Jake was suffering and she had to do something. And that she felt better after asking God to help.

Her attention divided between her thoughts, Alexa and Jake, and whether God cared about her lost memories, Gemma shivered when a chilly wind washed over her. She began climbing down the bleachers to retrieve her sweater from Jake's truck.

That's when the flashback hit.

Machu Picchu. Gemma knew it instantly, recognized the path she'd taken to the exact spot where she now saw herself standing. She knew the exact words she'd say to her tour group. Everything was so familiar.

Then suddenly the ground was moving and she couldn't find firm footing on it. Everything wobbled and tilted. Great gaping cracks opened up. Terror grabbed her by the throat as she ordered her guests to take cover against the side of the mountain. But she couldn't hide. She had to find Kurt. She screamed his name and moments later saw him just below her on a crumbling step. His eyes locked with hers and he mouthed something.

I love you, Gemma.

Then he was gone, his voice drowned out by a loud rumbling behind her. Rocks and debris tumbled down from above, piling around her feet. Someone grabbed her arm and yanked her forward in the same moment as she turned. Fierce pain radiated from the back of her head and blinded her.

Then the memory was over and she was huddled on the bleachers, shaking.

"Gemma! Gemma, wake up. You're okay. You're safe."

"Jake?" She blinked and found him peering down at her, his face haggard. Alexa was there, too, white-faced and scared. "I remember Kurt," she whispered. "I remember the earthquake."

Tears came then, oceans of sadness, filling her eyes, dripping down her cheeks and soaking her clothes. There was nothing she could do to stop them.

"Is Gem okay?" Alexa whispered.

"She's going to be fine, sweetheart. She just needs to rest. Let's get her to my truck." Jake scooped her into his arms and carried her across to the parking lot. Tenderly he set her in the vehicle before his fingers closed over hers. "Relax, Gem. You're safe now."

"Kurt knew he was going to die," she whispered, unable to stop the words from streaming out. "He knew and all he could think of was me. He kept repeating that he loved me. He loved me."

She remembered feeling that love, the safety and security of it, the certain knowledge that she wasn't alone, that she didn't have to be afraid because Kurt was there, that he would take care of her because she belonged with him. In the awareness of that knowledge came the understanding that she'd sought for that security her entire life, and that when she had finally found it, she'd been desperately afraid of losing it.

And now she had lost it, because now she belonged to no one, belonged nowhere.

"I'm alone."

She couldn't tell if she said it out loud or in her heart.

It didn't matter. It was still true.

Chapter Six

As soon as Eli's soccer practice ended, Jake drove to Olivia's ranch. He was desperate to get Gemma home to The Haven, as if that would somehow ease the agony of her memories. Eli and Alexa talked quietly in the back seat, perhaps sensing that Gemma needed space to process her thoughts. Jake guessed she was trying to make sense of her memories, though how much she'd actually recalled wasn't clear to him.

What was clear was the fury he felt at the words she'd whispered.

I'm alone.

Gemma *wasn't* alone. She had friends,

family, tons of people who loved and cared about her. The plethora of cards, letters and bouquets from well-wishers proved that, even though Gemma had left everything stacked in the office because reading the names and trying to remember the senders stressed her.

But she was not alone. She had him.

Jake immediately revised that. They were friends. He'd always had a soft spot for Gemma, yes. He'd also always known that friendship was all there could be. So he'd do whatever he could to help her now—everything but let his heart get over-involved. Because no matter how much he cared about her, he could not step beyond those invisible bonds. He'd promised Lily.

Anyway, Gemma only wanted a friend. So that's what he'd be.

"I'm going inside with you and Eli," she said when they arrived at Olivia's.

"Are you sure?" He'd hoped they'd drop off Eli and then leave. Jake immediately dropped that plan when he saw her chin jut out in determination.

"I want to hold her baby," Gemma insisted.

Alexa asked Eli to show her the birdhouses he'd been talking about, leaving Jake and Gemma to enter the house alone. When Olivia placed Mirella in Gemma's arms, Gemma's complete focus rested on her niece. Jake used the opportunity to take Olivia aside and explain what had happened.

"She seems okay now, just enthralled." Olivia smiled at her sister's rapt expression. "Which I totally understand because Gem always liked kids."

"Maybe your daughter is triggering more memories, Liv." Frustration gnawed at Jake. "There's no schedule or plan to this memory thing of hers. All I can do is assume she knows what she's doing."

"She always did," Olivia agreed, grinning. "Sit. Have a cup of coffee while Gemmie admires my beautiful daughter. Tell me what you've been up to in your community work."

"You name it, I'm trying to do it. Or get it done. I'm up to my ears," Jake confessed. "The list of needy folks never shrinks. It's a good thing the aunties aren't obsessive about my work schedule."

"You know they love having you at The Haven. You've been their lifesaver, especially when we girls couldn't get home to help them." Olivia plucked a list off the fridge. "As I mentioned last Sunday, I noted some folks I believe could use your help. None of them need physical assistance. In my opinion they're mostly lonely."

"Long list," he muttered.

"Since you have such a knack for building community connections between people, I thought you might know someone who could pay them a visit." Olivia's smile warmed his heart. "You provide a wonderful service, Jake."

"A service? All I wanted to do was keep folks in this community caring about each

other, though I'm not really qualified for it," he confessed.

"Your qualifications are that you care about our community." Olivia touched his cheek with her fingertip. "That's more than lots of people do and we're all grateful for what you do." She began loading the dishwasher.

Sure he cared, Jake mused. But there was getting to be way more than one man could do in his spare time to help folks.

Jake sat at the kitchen island, nursing his coffee as he thought about it. For a guy who'd tried hard to avoid getting involved, he was becoming pretty heavily vested in the locals' welfare. Not that it was personal. It was just…helping. Yet that weak word didn't fully express what he wanted to achieve. Maybe because he hadn't clearly defined it in his own mind? Maybe because he was trying to help in a personal way without getting personally involved.

Jake figured his crazy yen to fix things for

folks who couldn't do it themselves probably stemmed from years of watching the
aunts reach out to anyone who needed them.
They'd often drawn him in, too. It hadn't
taken him long to recognize that the elderly
ladies were swamped and wearing thin. So
he'd pitched in. And then he couldn't *not* help
because reaching out to folks brought sanity
to his life more than it helped anyone else.
He felt like it was one way he could atone
for causing Lily's and Thomas's deaths.

Cheap atonement. It didn't cost Jake anything but a couple of pieces of lumber to turn
Mr. Gertz's stairs into a ramp so he could get
in and out more easily. No need to bother the
aunties about visiting Billy or lots of other
shut-ins around Chokecherry Hollow either.
Nor did it take a genius to see single-mom
Nancy Filmore needed help fixing her ram-
shackle home, though Jake wasn't certain
that what he was doing was enough. Same
thing with Alexa. The kid needed someone

to give some stability to her world, but *him*? And how was he supposed to help Gem?

By not getting too involved.

At least his meager efforts to help others hadn't required talking to God. That gave Jake the freedom to tamp down his past and the *why* questions that would not be silenced. The ones God never answered.

Recently, however, he'd begun to feel less and less capable of helping others and more aware that he needed to help himself. Oh, he still saw the issues around him. He just wasn't certain he was making enough of a difference anymore. And now too many folks were looking to him to remedy their issues.

Jake was breaking his own rule. He was getting too involved.

So he'd try to scale back. But the one person Jake had to help was Gemma. She needed her life back.

"She's such a beautiful child," Gemma whispered, drawing his focus to her.

The myriad of expressions floating across her face—curiosity, joy and pleasure—all seemed to jumble together as she touched the tiny fingers, brushed her thumb against the baby's tipped-up nose and breathed in her scent.

"She'll make a great mother," Olivia murmured. Jake thought so, too.

Then Gemma lifted her head and smiled at him.

"What kind of a mind must God have to create such a miracle?" she breathed.

"A mind that is far greater than we can think or understand," Olivia murmured.

"Agreed." Because Mirella began to fuss, Gemma brushed a featherlight kiss against the baby's cheek before she handed her back to Olivia. "Thank you for sharing her," she murmured. "Does it feel strange to be a mother?"

"Sort of." Olivia snuggled her baby with a chuckle. "But remember, Gemmie, I've been waiting for her for a while. Would you like some coffee?"

"No, thank you. This is Alexa's first day at The Haven. I think we need to get her back so she can settle in." Gemma's wide smile spread as she watched the children through the patio doors. "She's had a busy day."

"Come again, anytime," Olivia invited them. "Mirella and I would love to see you."

"You have a beautiful place. I will come back." Gemma seemed bemused as she walked with Jake to the truck and climbed in. She waited while he buckled Alexa into her seat, hands folded in her lap, her eyes gazing at something he couldn't see.

"Are you all right?" he asked when they were halfway to The Haven.

"I think so." Gemma said nothing more until they arrived at the big house. Once there, she politely said thank you before they walked inside. She shared a few words with the aunts while Alexa gave him a hug that made his throat choke up.

"I love you, Jake," she whispered in his ear. Then she followed Gemma up the stairs, wondering aloud if her suitcase was already there.

When they'd disappeared, Jake gently closed the kitchen door and faced the aunts.

"Gemma remembered the earthquake and losing Kurt," he told them.

"She did seem rather quiet. It must be so confusing for her," Tillie said thoughtfully.

"Perhaps we'll go and help settle Alexa," Margaret said. "No doubt it's been a difficult day for our dear Gemma."

The ladies disappeared to help their foster daughter. Because Jake wasn't sure if Gemma would need to speak to him again tonight, he went out to wait on the back patio and got lost studying the twinkling stars.

"The Big Dipper's very clear tonight," she murmured a few moments later from behind him.

Jake rose. "Are you all right, Gem?"

"I'm fine." She sat down in the chair beside his. "I told Alexa a story about when I first went to Europe alone. That seemed to help her relax."

"Your stories never made me sleepy," he teased. "They made me want to go there." He tried to read her mood and figure out if the memory of the earthquake had rattled her. "Can I do anything for you?"

Please let me do something so I won't feel so useless.

"Thank you for offering, but what is there to do, Jake? Everything's the same as it was, only now I can remember," she mumbled.

"Everything?" he asked as he sat down beside her.

"No." When she shook her head, her gorgeous hair shivered in the moonlight. She pushed the rosy strands behind her ears before facing him. "I remember the earthquake. I remember Kurt's face and that he said he loved me. But that's it. Only bits and pieces of other stuff."

"You were wrong, you know." He needed to say it, even if it did shock her.

"I was?" Her green eyes widened.

"You said you're alone. You're not." He had to erase those thoughts so her brain would be open to embrace the next set of memories. "You're among family, people who love you."

"I think I've always been alone." The pathos in her whisper gutted him. "I think that if I asked the aunts, they'd tell me that I never had a family—no mother, no father, no siblings. I'm just…here," she said after a short pause. "By myself."

"I'm here. Your aunts are upstairs with Alexa. Your sisters are nearby," he argued.

"Yes." She didn't debate him.

"You are loved and surrounded by those who love you. What does your past matter?" he demanded in frustration.

"What was your childhood like, Jake?" Her whispered appeal begged him to answer.

"Happy, I guess. My parents owned a nursery and I grew up among the plants, which I loved." He shrugged. "Mom got breast cancer when I eight. She died when I was twelve and Dad missed her terribly. When I finished school, he sold his business but kept on working for the new owners. He died of heart failure a year after I left home."

"I'm sorry. No brothers and sisters? Cousins?" she murmured.

"My parents were only children. There was no one else. Until—" *No! Don't go there.*

"Until Lily," Gemma murmured, a tender smile turning up her lips. "I think that's how it was with me, Jake. Kurt was my anchor when there was no one else."

"You had your aunts, your foster sisters," he protested.

"*We* had *our* aunts, *our* foster sisters," she corrected. "It's not the same as having someone special of your own."

"Gemma—"

"The thing I don't understand is why Kurt loved me like that." Her forehead wrinkled as she struggled to express herself. "What I saw—he knew he would die, Jake. And yet his focus stayed on me, on making sure I knew he loved me. I can't absorb that. It was life and death. Why wasn't he worried about his own safety? Why didn't he call for help? At that particular point, what did loving me matter?"

"You were the only thing that mattered to Kurt." Jake leaned back in his chair, smiling at the cascade of memories of Gemma's husband. "That was always obvious."

"It was?" She frowned.

"Yes, because that's who Kurt was. A man who loved others. Nothing mattered to him as much as people, especially you, Gem." Jake smiled at her. "Love was the reason he had to make that trust for Alexa. Because she mattered to him. I've never known anyone with a bigger heart than Kurt Andrews."

"He sounds nice. I wish I could fully remember him." Gemma squinted as a star flashed through the sky. "Every time I say his name I see Christmas cards. It's really weird."

Jake shouted with laughter which he quickly muted because of their guests.

"What's so funny?" Gemma asked.

"Christmas cards. Surely you remember that list of Kurt's? Every year he'd send a photo card to everyone on his list. It had maybe a couple hundred names of people, including the folks who'd been on every one of his tours. He was nuts about ensuring people knew he remembered them." Jake glanced at her. "You once told me that's why he had so many return clients, that they loved his personal touches."

Jake had always envied Kurt, partly for his sunny disposition and the way he'd lavished himself on other people, partly because it seemed so easy for him to give love, and partly because he gave of himself wholeheartedly, without reservation. Mostly because he genuinely loved Gem. Kurt hadn't had anything to atone for.

"Did I love my husband, Jake?" Gemma whispered.

"What?" He blinked his surprise at her doubt, but given her pleading gaze, he knew she was serious. "Yes, you loved him."

"Oh." Her head bowed.

"Why did you ask that, Gem?"

"Because I don't feel anything. It's like I'm a shadow, not really here. I'm dead inside. Or frozen." She glanced over one shoulder, as if to check if anyone was near. "My aunts. They're wonderful, giving women who've tried their best to make me feel at home. They're amazing ladies."

"They are," Jake agreed. "But?"

"But I don't *feel* love. I *like* them, but…" Her voice trailed away on a sigh.

"Love seldom comes immediately to anyone, Gemma," Jake said. "You've just met the ladies. You don't know them well yet. Given time, you will love them just as everyone else does. You won't be able to help it. That's the way love works."

"Maybe." She didn't sound convinced.

"It's like faith." Jake stopped. He was hardly the right person to be talking about faith. He'd avoided communication with God since Lily and Thomas had died. "Not that I'm any expert."

"You mean, the more we pray, the better we get to know God?" she asked.

"Maybe that's what I'm trying to say. Badly." It was late. Gemma needed her rest. So did he, if only to stop himself from spouting any more homilies.

Apparently Gemma thought so, too, because after several moments of contemplation, she rose, smoothed her wind-tossed hair off her face and smiled at him.

"Everything is going round and round in my head." Tiredness leached into the words. "I hear you, but nothing computes in my brain. I *should* love those two old ladies, if only because they have loved me and raised me, given me a wonderful home here at The Haven."

"Are you sure you don't?" Jake asked.

"I'm not sure I know what love is. Everything is so mixed-up, so confused and out of place. Nothing seems quite real." She exhaled on a long sigh. "I can't figure out what I feel, Jake. Or maybe I'm afraid to."

"Afraid?" He stared at her. "What are you afraid of, Gem?"

Minutes yawned between them.

"That I'll disappoint them," she whispered, her voice ragged. "That I won't fulfill their expectations, won't be the daughter they want."

Jake didn't move. He didn't make a sound because he knew there was more coming.

"The Gemma they knew disappeared in the earthquake," she said starkly. "I'm terrified I will never remember how to get her back."

Before Jake could reassure her she rushed away, leaving him alone in the night.

One by one the lights in the old stone house extinguished until only the exterior yard lights illuminated the vast grounds. Jake rose and stretched to ease the crick in his neck. He pulled his arms across his body to loosen the tautness in his shoulders. But no amount of stretching could dissolve the tight band in his gut. Gemma was hurting.

He walked the short distance to his cabin, but he didn't retire. There would be no rest for him tonight. His mind whirled with thoughts of Gemma and how he could make her see that she was who they claimed, that even if she had changed, she would still be Gemma, still loved, still cherished, still needed.

Sure, he could repeat stories about her past, tell her how she'd shown her heart of love a million ways. But they were just words. What Gemma wanted, needed, was inner certainty that she wasn't alone. That was not something he could give her.

As Jake sat on a bench outside his door, thinking, two young deer appeared and began grazing under the wavering spruce trees. Maybe it was because his barriers were down that his brain suddenly filled with memories of Lily, of their simple wedding and of her promise that nothing would ever come between them.

Promise me we won't ever let anything matter more than we do to each other, Jake.

How foolish he'd been. He'd let his work, business pressures and the pull of everyday life take precedence over the preciousness of his family. Of love. He knew that now, knew how easily one could forget the things that really mattered.

"But why did Lily and Thomas have to die for me to learn that? Why couldn't You have taken me instead?" he asked.

There was no answer. There never had been. That was why he had no answers for Gemma. Jake had no answers for himself.

In her darkened room, Gemma sat on the window seat in her room and stared across the valley. The full moon provided enough illumination for her to identify hills and knolls she'd probably tromped over in the past, but she couldn't remember now.

Two deer foraged for food near the perimeter of the woods. Mesmerized by the way their gazes darted from side to side between bites, she relived the warm, fluttery feelings of security when Jake had held her in his arms and carried her to the truck.

He'd held her as if she was precious cargo to be protected. He'd set her on the seat so gently, fussing to ensure her comfort, his face very serious, as if she was an important part of his world, someone he had a duty to care for.

Before he disappeared, Kurt had given her the same look, an intense, cherishing stare that said she was vital to him. But now Kurt was gone and Gemma couldn't feel anything but a sense of loss.

Was that because of his letter which the lawyer had given her? She'd read it earlier, confused by the way Kurt had ended it. His words were engraved on her brain.

I know I should have told you about Alexa before we were married, Gemma. Your aunts accused me of hiding her out of fear that you wouldn't accept her without knowing her. Perhaps that's true. In retrospect, I think you'd have understood because you have a truly loving heart. People matter as much to you as they do me. That's what bonds us, Gem.

I love Alexa. From the first time I saw her, I felt compelled to be the father she doesn't have. Please, please, darling, now that I'm gone, take up that duty for me. Make sure she's safe and happy, but most of all loved. Teach her about God, how He loves us. How He's always there, always caring for us no matter whether we can see Him working or not. Then, when she's missing me, when she cries because I'm not there to hug her, she will remember your assurance that no mat-

ter what happens, God is on the job. Take care of Alexa for me, sweetheart.

I love you, Kurt.

God is on the job? Then what was He doing when the earthquake happened? Where was He when the earth swallowed Kurt and left her brain empty of everything that mattered? Gemma couldn't accept Kurt's words because she couldn't make them make sense.

Why? The word resounded in her head over and over.

Gemma was tired and so weary of trying to figure out herself. The answers to who she was wouldn't come and that left her more frustrated. Now she had a child to consider. What was she to do with Alexa? It was fine to give her a holiday here at The Haven, but then what? Send her back to foster care? She hated that thought, but what had Kurt expected her to do with the little girl?

If only she could sleep, let the cares and worries roll away in sweet oblivion without the recurring nightmare of the earthquake invading her rest. Defeated, yet knowing she needed to rest, she began to rise but paused when she spotted a lone figure walking around the garden enclosure.

Jake. She recognized the relaxed way he strode over the uneven ground, never faltering or stumbling. Apparently he couldn't rest either. Gemma thought she knew why. Lily and Thomas. Such a sad story.

Was God working then, too?

Fed up with her thoughts, she turned down her bed. Her glance rested on the framed cross-stitch picture on the wall, illuminated by a shaft of moonlight.

And we know that all things work together for good to them that love God, to them who are the called according to His purpose. Romans 8:28

All things work together for good—Kurt's death? Alexa's mom's death? Lily and Thomas dying? How could any of that be made into good?

Frustrated by the lack of answers, Gemma

made a mental note. Come morning, she'd ask the aunties about it. Then maybe she'd be able to offer Jake solace.

Chapter Seven

The next morning Jake paused outside at the corner of the house because he heard the aunties speaking. Sensing the importance of their words in the quiet solemnity of the early morning, he stayed where he was, loathe to interrupt but curious.

"We've always felt that cross-stitch picture wasn't finished, dear," Tillie said.

"Yes, because who wants to hear that verse when they're in pain or grieving? 'All things work together for good,'" Aunt Margaret said with a frown. "It doesn't help you much, does it? You're still hurting terribly. You want to know why."

"Exactly," Gemma agreed.

Jake heard a note of hopelessness in her response.

"The thing is, God doesn't leave us hanging like that. Verse 28 is only half the thought," Tillie explained. "You have to link it with verse 29 to completely understand what's meant."

Jake had never heard this before. Though Romans 8:28 had been recited to him many times after Lily's and Thomas's deaths, he'd always resented the words. As if their horrible deaths were somehow good. Now, intrigued by the ladies' explanations, he leaned a shoulder against the stone wall, prepared to hear their clarification.

"You see, dear, the very reason for verse 28 *is* verse 29," Margaret explained. "God *does* work all things together for good according to His purpose. But what is that purpose? Verse 29 tells us that God is making us more like His Son."

"Let me put it this way." Tillie's chuckle

warmed a spot in Jake's heart. "After we become Christians, why doesn't God send us to heaven and thereby save us the heartache and pain we feel? Then we'd avoid all the bad stuff in life."

Jake had often wondered the same thing.

"God doesn't rescue us and spirit us away because He wants us to exercise our faith, to depend on His power and thereby develop maturity and strength. To become like Jesus," she finished.

"If you never face adversity and figure out how to get through it with God, you won't grow as a Christian or develop enough depth to withstand the next storm in life," Margaret agreed. "And there are always storms, my dear."

"You're saying that this memory-failure thing of mine…" Gemma's words came slowly, thoughtfully. "That God is somehow using it to make me like Jesus?"

"Yes!" the ladies exclaimed together.

"So what you're really telling me is that no

suffering is wasted." She sounded stunned by her conclusion.

Jake was, too. Except in his case it was worse. It meant Lily and Thomas had died because of him. But then, he already knew that.

"To help us through this suffering, verse 28 assures us that we *know*. We don't think or hope or feel," Tillie emphasized. "We *know*, even if we can't understand how or why or when, we know that God is going to benefit us."

God was using Lily's and Thomas's deaths to *benefit* him? Jake couldn't see how. Apparently Gemma felt the same.

"How could my not remembering anything help me?" she demanded.

"We don't know. It's God's plan, not ours," Margaret said crisply.

"Maybe it's to help you learn things about yourself you otherwise would not have learned," Tillie suggested. "Or maybe it's to help you help others. You may never know.

The thing to hang on to is the Bible's promise that God is working for your good." Confidence laced her words.

"Also, remember Psalms tells us God puts our tears in a bottle. In Isaiah it says we are inscribed on the palms of His hands. He knows every detail of our suffering." Margaret's smile infused her voice. "You're not suffering pointlessly, Gemma. God hasn't abandoned you."

"Even if I can deal with that, what's next?" Gemma sounded hesitant. "Where do I go from here? What am I supposed to *do*?"

"Darling, we'd like to tell you that, but *we* don't have the answers. You need to seek God, wait for His direction," Tillie said.

Jake peeked around the corner of the building. The aunts were seated on either side of their foster daughter, hands clasped, heads bent together.

"For right now, do whatever you can to make a difference in someone's world. Pitch in wherever and whenever you can to help others. God will show you His way, dear, but it may take time." Margaret patted her shoulder. "Perhaps you can use that time to spend with Alexa."

"I'm just supposed to keep living here, doing nothing?" Gemma's indignant voice rose. "I'm sponging off you."

"No. You're spending time with your family," Tillie corrected. "And we love that. Why not just enjoy it while you wait for God's next move?"

"I understand now why Jake said I'd love you." Tears muffled Gemma's words. "You don't judge, you don't chastise, you don't push. You just..." She paused as if searching for exactly the right word. "Love."

"That's what Jesus did. That's what God tells us to do, and we do love you, dear. Very much." Margaret brushed the wind-tossed strands off her face. "Now rest in God's promise as you begin reforming your life. He is at work."

"I believe I hear your little Alexa calling."

Tillie chuckled. "Spending time with her is going to keep you very busy."

"Yes, it will. Thank you, Aunties." Gemma rose and walked inside.

"You can come out now, Jake," Margaret called.

He felt his face burn to the roots of his hairline as he stepped around the corner.

"I'm sorry. I wasn't trying to eavesdrop," he hurriedly assured them. "What you were saying intrigues me though."

"Because of your family." Tillie nodded. "You suffer greatly over their loss."

"You're like our Gemmie, fussing about the past and the outcome of your troubles instead of learning the lessons." Margaret's disapproving face chastised him.

"Lessons? Outcome?" He shook his head. "I don't have an outcome. I'm just a handy-man."

Tillie sputtered with laughter.

"My dear Jake, you are a child of the most high God." A very serious-faced Margaret studied him. "Do you know the first things children do when they get hurt?"

He shook his head, not wanting to remember Thomas hurting.

"They lift their arms to be picked up and comforted," Tillie said. "They're humble. They don't let pride or anger get in the way. If they need food, changing, comfort, they reach for it. We need to do the same because God's hands are always outstretched toward us."

"Rather like yours are to the people of this community," Margaret murmured, her intense gaze searching his. "Perhaps it's time you allowed someone to hold *your* hand and comfort *you*, Jake."

Excusing themselves, the ladies bustled off to a day filled with ministering to others. Jake intended to find a solitary place and think about what they'd said until Gemma's voice stopped him.

"Good morning, Jake. Can Alexa and I help you with anything?"

"Good morning." He studied her face, saw need. "Have you already run out of ideas to entertain her?"

"According to Alexa, I'm not very knowledgeable when it comes to a four-almost-five-year-old." Auburn waves flowed over her shoulders as she gazed at him with what he interpreted as shame darkening her green eyes.

"Me, neither. I guess we'll learn together. I have some odd jobs around here that I need to complete this morning, but you can't help with those," he said.

"The bank wants me to go see them. I guess I could take Alexa with me. That would fill in an hour or so," Gemma mumbled. "But I can't think of what to do with her this afternoon. She doesn't seem interested in joining any of the kids' groups."

The look of distress on her face made Jake mentally revise his schedule.

"This afternoon I need to visit a single mom who has three kids and laundry problems."

"Not a good combination." Gemma made a face.

"No. Want to come along?" He wasn't sure what Gemma would do, but at least she and Alexa would get some social interaction.

"That would be great." Relief washed across her sculptured features. "Maybe later this morning I'll take Alexa with the group who's going horse riding at Adele's ranch. Alexa said she's never done that."

"Sounds like a plan." Jake grinned when she waggled her fingers and almost skipped into the house. Looked like the former, bubbly Gemma was on her way back. Had the aunties' advice helped her?

As Jake dealt with Sweetie the cow, mowed the front lawns and tilled the flower beds, he struggled to make sense of what the aunts had said.

How was it possible for the deaths of his beloved family to make him more like Jesus?

Maybe, for the first time, the aunts were wrong.

* * *

"So, tell me about this single mom." Having settled Alexa with her phone and earbuds so she could listen to music, Gemma waited expectantly.

"Her name is Nancy Fillmore. Last year she came home after having given birth to her third child to find a note from her husband." Jake's teeth automatically gritted. "He'd abandoned them. The idiot has no idea what he's thrown away."

"But—why?" Gemma gasped.

"Said he couldn't take the responsibility. So Nancy was left alone with three kids to support while recovering from a C-section."

"What a rat!" Gemma gaped at him, shocked by the new dad's actions.

"Nancy had no time to think about that. Her maternity leave was extended because of the surgery so at least she's been able to stay home and help her kids adjust," Jake explained.

"Wait. Let me guess." Gemma pursed her

lips, considered what she'd learned about Jake and said, "You got the community involved to help her."

"Nope. That would have embarrassed Nancy. She's very proud. She didn't want anyone to know she was struggling. I wasn't sure what to do until Adele said Nancy needed to feel cared for." He shrugged. "She and Liv organized a baby shower. Victoria said new clothes would help Nancy. Your sisters brainstormed a little more and eventually came up with the idea that folks could give gift cards so Nancy could get whatever she needed."

"Smart ladies, my sisters." Gemma applauded proudly.

"Things kind of snowballed after that." Jake chuckled. "Your aunts got into the act by arranging for Nancy's two eldest children to attend summer camp at The Haven. That gave her time to adjust to single motherhood. Now she's managing."

"Wow." Gemma gazed at Jake appreciatively. "And you were the one who got the ball rolling. Good job. So why are we going to her house now?"

"Nancy is getting her life on track, but her house isn't." Jake seemed to hesitate.

"Whatever you tell me will remain confidential," Gemma assured him. He'd never divulged many details of what he did for the townsfolk, but maybe that was because he wasn't sure he could trust her. "I'm not a gossip."

"I know that, Gem." Jake's smile sent a current of warmth through her. "Fortunately Nancy doesn't have much of a mortgage because her great-aunt left her the house. But it's very old. Even if Nancy returned to nursing full-time, her salary wouldn't be enough to cover needed improvements."

"What are we talking about?" she asked curiously.

"Basic stuff. A new roof, new windows and replacement of the rest of her nearly dead appliances, including a new furnace. Paint. Minor repairs on just about everything else." His grimace revealed the direness of the situation.

"How are we going to help her today?" Gemma liked that this seemed like an opportunity to do something, to be part of something instead of waiting on the sidelines to remember a tidbit of her past. "What can I do?"

"From time to time folks give me—uh, let's call them anonymous donations to use to help somebody," he said carefully. "Today, thanks to a donation, Nancy is getting a new washer and dryer, and trust me, she desperately needs both. With a baby and two little kids, she can't afford the time, money or energy to keep running to the laundromat."

"You have a wonderful ministry, Jake." Gemma fell silent for several moments before asking, "Can anyone contribute to your work?"

"Sure." His face revealed his puzzlement. "Why?"

"Mr. Hornby asked me to go to the bank

because Kurt's insurance has been settled. Apparently there were several policies, including a very generous one from his—our employer. It's in an account in my name." Gemma studied Jake. "From what everyone's told me about Kurt, I think he'd like to know some of his money is being used to help others."

Jake pulled into Nancy's yard, stopped his truck and stared at her.

"That's amazingly generous of you, Gemma," he finally said. "But you should keep that money for yourself, for your future."

"I don't need it. Apparently I was also a very good saver. At least that's what the accounts the aunts helped me transfer here from Toronto show. And I'm living free at The Haven." Her voice softened. "Trust me, there's more than enough money for anything in my future." He still looked dubious so she added, "I want to share in helping Nancy, even if it's only with money." She told him how much money she wanted to contribute.

She wasn't going to tell him the rest of her newly forming plan. No yet. Not till she'd thought it through.

"If you're sure, then thank you, Gemma." Jake's grin was all the thanks she needed. "You just fixed another problem. I have a pensioner who can't afford a refrigerator. She's been living without one for months. This will be an answer her prayers."

"Living without a fridge?" She couldn't imagine it. "That's awful."

"It was easier when the weather was colder, but now you've settled my concern about the summer. She'll get a new fridge to keep her medication cool thanks to you." Jake's face shone and his eyes glowed with excitement. He was so handsome. "If you're willing, you can be an even bigger part of things for the next few hours."

"Okay?" She blinked. "How?"

"Keep Nancy's kids busy while the old appliances are removed and the new ones are installed. Of course, that can only happen after the flooring people replace her wrecked linoleum," he explained with a grin. "Might take the whole afternoon."

"Good. Alexa and I will do whatever we can to help." Slightly abashed, Gemma gulped but hid her inner worry about failing.

"Just give me a minute to phone the appliance store to see if they can deliver Mrs. Burns a fridge today. Then I'll introduce you to Nancy."

While Jake spoke on the phone, Gemma thought about all the money from Kurt's estate. She was his beneficiary on the policies, but she didn't want that money. It would feel somehow wrong to hoard it when she already had so much of her own, though she had no idea where it had all come from. She'd learned she had numerous stocks and bonds and other investments. She'd study the papers in her purse when she was alone tonight, see if she could figure it out. Tour guides must be much higher paid than she'd imagined.

She'd already instructed Mr. Hornby to increase Alexa's trust fund, and now ideas to use even more percolated. She could help Jake with his community work in a way that really mattered.

"They can deliver the fridge today," Jake said, pocketing his phone. "Come on, Gem. Let's go meet Nancy."

The new mom welcomed Gemma and Alexa, introduced her kids and then showed them where the new washer and dryer would go.

"Jake's been such a sweetheart to help us out," she told Gemma, eyes brimming with pride as she watched her two eldest children invite Alexa to play in the sandbox Jake had built. "I can't imagine how I'd have made it through without him."

Gemma muttered some response she hoped was appropriate, but her focus was on Nancy's eldest, Jeremy, whose face was distorted by a harelip. She knew there was surgery available to correct such an issue. Why hadn't Nancy had it done? She couldn't want her child to go through life so disfigured.

Alexa tugged on her skirt. She beckoned Gemma to bend down.

"That boy," she whispered, when Nancy was busy with the baby. "His face is hurted. Isn't nobody gonna fix it for him?"

"I don't know, sweetheart. But let's not mention it, okay?" She smiled to soften the words. "It might hurt his feelings and we don't want to do that."

"Nope. But when he goes to school, the other kids are gonna call him names." Alexa nodded wisely as if she'd experienced the phenomenon herself. "Sometimes kids aren't nice," she proclaimed. Lips pressed together, she rejoined the other kids.

Gemma stood mesmerized by a scene in her head. A circle of boys yelled *carrot top* at her while they ran round and round, refusing to allow her to escape. The shame, embarrassment and pain hit like a physical blow in the pit of her stomach. Alexa was right. Jeremy would suffer from the other kids' teasing. Kids always picked on the weakest one, the most different one, the *orphaned* one.

When she'd asked yesterday, the aunts had told her she'd been an orphan. Meaning she'd once had a family of some kind, but they were gone. That's why she'd been in foster care. She'd been suddenly afraid to ask more. And yet the lack of knowledge stymied her. These little flashbacks were so annoying, but apparently being teased about her hair was the only memory her brain would release today.

While Jake and Nancy discussed removing the old appliances, Gemma went to find the back door and the children. She was appalled by the state of the house. Old wooden windows didn't close properly. They'd be a nightmare in the winter. The heating bill must be through the roof. How did you keep kids healthy in a drafty old place like this? The back screen door was propped open because it was broken and the glass in the door had long ago cracked. The kitchen appliances looked like relics from the 1950s, though they sparkled clean and bright. The house was immaculate, but no amount of cleaning could disguise tattered floorboards showing through the ancient linoleum.

And then Gemma saw the quilts. Three of them, hanging in a small room in the corner. Drawn by their beautiful designs and gorgeous colors, she moved closer, fingering the fabrics as she studied the delicate stitches that held each together. Hand-quilted.

"I see you found my weakness," Nancy laughed.

"I'm so sorry. I didn't mean to pry. I was looking for Alexa—these are amazing," she interrupted herself to exclaim. "You did all this?"

"My great-aunt raised me," Nancy explained, waving a hand. "She was an extraordinary quilter. She taught me to love it, too. So whenever I have a spare moment, I come here and let my brain daydream."

"Your dreams are stunning." Gemma let go of the fabric. That's when she noticed a detailed wall hanging depicting happy children playing in the snow, two appliqued pillows and three backpacks with puffy faces and bright eyes that stared at her. Each item was unique. Gemma couldn't stop staring. "You're very talented, Nancy."

"It's my passion," the other woman breathed, a misty fondness in her eyes. "I've had to resort to completely hand stitching everything though."

"Why?" Dazed by the beauty she saw, Gemma thought this woman should never stop creating.

"My great-aunt's sewing machine is broken and this time I can't cobble it together. I think it needs a specific part that is probably either obsolete or crazy expensive."

She laughed and shrugged it off. "Can I get you coffee?"

Just then someone rapped on the front door.

"No coffee, thank you, Nancy. I'll go find the kids and keep them busy while the workmen do their jobs."

Asked about the baby, Nancy told her Sophie was now fast asleep. Gemma went outside and when the children grew restless, she took them for a walk to the park to enjoy the playground equipment.

But she couldn't forget that sewing room. Or the amazing talent that had been silenced for lack of a part on an old machine.

The afternoon flew past. When the floor had been installed and the appliances, gleaming and bright, were finally in their places, the washer already running, Jake ordered pizza while Nancy made a huge pitcher of fresh lemonade.

The warm day had cooled by the time they returned to The Haven, with Nancy's thanks ringing in their ears. Alexa had fallen fast asleep in the back seat. Gemma knew exactly what she wanted to do next. But first she needed information.

"Why doesn't Nancy get surgery for Jeremy?" she asked. "It should be done before he starts school, so he'll be like the other kids. Does she need money for that?"

"No, time." Jake smiled at her surprise. "The doctors in Edmonton will do it as part of their health care, but she will have to stay with him for between ten days and two weeks. Nancy can't afford that."

"But there are places which offer almost free lodging. Anyway, does she have to be there the entire time?" Gemma wondered.

"Nancy would never leave Jeremy by himself." Jake heaved a sigh. "But she also can't take the other two along—especially Sophie—and she doesn't want to ask anyone to babysit if she can't pay them properly. I've been trying to work out something, but so far…"

He didn't finish. When they arrived at The Haven, he returned Alexa's hug, smiling as she hurried toward the aunties.

"Well, guess I've got chores to do." He grinned at her. "Thank you for all your help, Gem. You are a blessing."

"My pleasure." She frowned, wondered if he'd accept her idea. "When you've got some time, say later tonight around nine thirty, will you meet me on the patio?"

"Sure. Why?" He frowned as he stared at her. "What do you need?"

"Help," she said simply. "See you later."

Her mind brimming with plans, Gemma ate with Alexa, supervised her bath and then tucked her into bed. Alexa wouldn't sleep until she got another story about Gemma's travels.

"Will you take me there someday?" she asked, barely smothering a yawn. "I'd like to see the kids in those costumes you talked about. And hear them sing."

"We'll plan on it," Gemma promised.

"Good night, sweetie." She savored the little girl's fierce hug and brushed a kiss over her brow, her heart welling with love. *Thank you for Alexa, Kurt,* she whispered inside her head.

Then Gemma retired to her room to make a list. That had always been the way she thought best.

When she was finished, she leaned back with a satisfied smile.

Jake had no idea what he'd unleashed today.

Chapter Eight

Three weeks later Jake once more sat outside Nancy's home with Gemma, this time in her brand-new car.

"Are you sure about this?" he asked, trying to hide his concerns. There was so much involved…

"We can do this, Jake. You're the detail man and you've organized everything. I'm the sitter. If I need help with the kids, I can call on my sisters or my aunts. I have a vehicle to transport the children to their activities. I have their car seats. I can do this," she said, her megawatt grin blazing. "Can you?" she asked, one golden-red eyebrow raised.

"I sure hope so." Truthfully, he wasn't certain they could carry off this magnificent plan of hers. But he was determined to try.

"Then let's get Nancy and Jeremy on their way to the hospital in Edmonton. Nothing can happen until they're out of here," Gemma reminded.

"True." Jake exited the car with a heart full of admiration for her intentions, but a gut full of worry about all the things that could go wrong with her incredible plan.

"We prayed about this, remember?" Her big green eyes dared him to voice one doubt. "Are you going to trust God or not?"

As rebukes went, it was a good one. Jake shut down his nagging uncertainties and grinned.

"Well?" she demanded.

"Lead on, Gem. You're in charge."

"And don't you forget it," she shot back and then spoiled the smartness of that remark with a wink.

Half an hour later, after an abundance of

directions and many hugs—some tearful—
Nancy and Jeremy were on their way. Ten
minutes after that, just as Jake finished loading the children's suitcases in Gemma's car,
a hoard of tradesmen began arriving.

"You're sure the kids will be okay over-
nighting at The Haven?" He eyed Sophie
and Donnie dubiously. "I doubt they've ever
slept anywhere else but here, and I don't remember you doing much babysitting in the
past—"

"Shh!" Gemma glared at him. "If this
place is livable, we'll come back and stay
the night. If not, we'll sleep at The Haven,"
she whispered. "You do your part and I'll
do mine." She raised her voice. "Right now
we're off to preschool. After that we're having lunch in the park."

"Sounds fun." He knew baby Sophie
wouldn't be a problem. She seemed most
adaptable. Donnie worried him. The kid
wasn't quite finished with the terrible twos
and didn't mind expressing his dissatisfac-

tion with his world—often loudly and sometimes for lengthy periods of time.

"This afternoon we're going to have ice cream in the park," Gemma said, apparently as aware as Jake of the glower on Donnie's face. "I'm having maple walnut. Sophie wants vanilla. Donnie's still deciding what flavor he'd like."

"I'd choose chocolate," Jake said. "With fudge topping and lots of sprinkles."

Donnie's mutinous expression turned thoughtful as Gemma buckled in the kids. Once she was in the driver's seat, she rolled down her window.

"You can do this, Jake," she said cheerily. "With God's help. See you later."

With God's help. He hadn't even asked for that. He stood there, staring at her disappearing car, thinking what a wonderful encourager Gemma was, until a major crash echoed inside Nancy's house.

"I know I haven't been talking to You regularly," he mumbled as he crossed the yard.

"And I have no right to ask anything. But this idea of Gem's—it's a massive undertaking and she's so gung ho on it. Could You please help us make it work?"

There was no clap of thunder or even an inner voice to guide him. Jake figured that meant God expected him to just get on with it.

"Why did you offer to do this, Jake?" he muttered when at noon his muscles loudly protested the hard work of removal. "Next time mind your own business."

"You talkin' to me?" the electrician asked.

"No." Jake clamped his lips together and concentrated on tearing out the kitchen cabinets that were probably installed long before Nancy's great-aunt had even been born.

"Two bathrooms and a kitchen reno, rewiring, replumbing, new flooring and painting the whole place, inside and out." Marcus the electrician rolled his eyes. "And you're expecting it to be done in ten days? You're dreaming, Jake."

"Maybe."

It didn't matter how hard it was. This was Gemma's dream. He would work his butt off to make it come true if only because Gemma was finally dreaming again. As a bonus her dream was going to totally change Nancy's life. Jake shrugged.

"Piece of cake, Marcus."

"Wow!" Two days later Gemma surveyed Nancy's now open-plan first floor, turning in a circle that made baby Sophie burble with laughter. "This is amazing, Jake."

"It's a mess," he corrected, his smug grin tugging up his downturned lips. "At least the tear-out went faster than I expected. We uncovered a few issues while installing those support beams, but there wasn't anything we couldn't handle."

Gemma only partly listened as he described eons-old cast iron plumbing pipes that had to be replaced, service lines he'd dug up so the tree roots could be removed and a host of other mechanical issues necessary to bring the old house into the modern era.

"We had ten men show up to help install the new windows and doors yesterday, so that got finished very quickly," Jake continued. "Do you like them?"

"I love them, especially those French doors to the backyard. Nancy will be able to see the kids when she's working in the kitchen." Gemma licked the tip of her finger and made an invisible number one then struck a pose. "Score one for me. I'm not just a useless former tour guide, you know."

"Never useless," he said. "You're a very generous woman who's making a mom's unspoken dreams come true. You are extraordinary, Gem. Paying for all this—it's really amazing."

"Shh!" She glanced around to be sure no workmen were nearby to overhear, while trying to disguise her pleasure at the praise Jake was heaping on her. "The money thing is between us, remember? As far as everyone else is concerned, an anonymous donation is paying for this."

"But if Nancy knew she would—"

"I don't want her to feel beholden every time she sees me." Gemma shook her head, her auburn mane rippling with the action. Sophie clamped chubby fingers around a hank of it and giggled. "I just want to be part of the team that helps make this come true." Gemma winced as she freed the strands from the baby's fingers. "A silent part."

"A very big part," Jake corrected.

"What's next?" she asked, intrigued by the process of renovating such an old house.

"Plasterers have been in once to begin repairs. They'll work overnight and probably finish tomorrow morning. When that's dry we'll paint. After that we can begin to put things back together."

"It's going to be lovely, isn't it? Just like Nancy and her kids." Gemma pressed a kiss to Sophie's cheek, loving the feel of the child's downy-soft skin. "And apparently Jeremy's surgery went well, too. The aunts told me."

"I heard that from Nancy this morning. Where's Alexa?" Jake laid out an array of paint colors.

"I begged the preschool place to let her attend while she's visiting." Gemma smirked, eager to share her secret. "She's helping Donnie fit in there."

"Yeah? Why would she do that?" Jake's knowing look made her blush. "What are you bribing her with?"

"Cowboy boots. Well, I have to buy them for her anyway," Gemma argued, blushing at the smirk on his face. "She loves riding."

"Uh-huh." Jake shook his head. "You're a pushover for a strong-willed kid like Alexa, Gem."

"Probably, but I need to make up to that little girl for all she's lost. If cowboy boots can help do that then I'm in." She didn't like the way his brow furrowed or the way he cleared his throat.

"I know you want to heal everyone's hurts, Gem, but please be careful."

"Of what?" she asked. But she knew what he'd say. "Don't love Alexa too much? Don't let her have a piece of my heart? I can't help it. Everything else in my world is upside down. I can't make sense of or remember most of it. But this bond Alexa and I are building—it's mine. It's something I don't have to try to remember. It's here and now. It's real. For you, too," she charged.

He opened his mouth to interrupt but she wouldn't let him.

"Admit it, Jake. You're crazy about that kid. Otherwise why would you have spent last evening, when you were stiff, sore and tired, showing her how to plant her flower garden?"

"I like Alexa very much." His face was so serious. "But we have to keep our feelings in check."

"Why?" she demanded.

"Because what happens when Alexa leaves?" he asked quietly.

"Hopefully we'll have built a connection we'll all cherish and we'll keep that going into our futures. Don't you think that's why Kurt asked me to watch out for her?" Gemma didn't want to hear Jake's warning. She sure didn't want to think about Alexa leaving or about being alone. Again. "It's almost time for Sophie's nap and I need to pick up Alexa and Donnie."

"What treat are you spoiling them with today?" he asked, one dark eyebrow lifted.

"I'm not spoiling them," she snapped. Then backtracked. "Okay, maybe a little bit. We're going to do some finger-painting and make pictures for their bedroom walls."

Jake shook his head as if stunned.

"What's that look for?" Gemma demanded.

"I'm amazed at the ideas that fill that pretty head of yours. I had no idea you would be such a fantastic surrogate mom." Something in his words made her look, really look at him. But she had to quickly avert her eyes because a nervous shiver made her knees weak when he added, "You're quite a lady, Gemma Andrews."

"Oh, phooey. I'm an ordinary female who likes kids and wants to keep them happy," she said, uncomfortable with his fulsome praise. "Don't make me out to be some kind of hero."

"I don't have to," Jake said very softly, his probing blue-eyed gaze holding hers. "It's just who you are."

She quickly turned the conversation to the paint samples, pretending to check that he'd ordered it in the shades she'd chosen.

"Nancy loves that pale turquoise that's so popular now," she explained. "You can see it in her quilts and cushions. And when her sofa's recovered, it's going to fit in perfectly against that pretty wallpaper." Gemma had no idea where this interior decorating knowledge came from. She only knew that every morning she prayed God would help her to choose things Nancy would like. And then she followed her heart.

"You're the boss." Jake tickled Sophie under her chin and chuckled when she reached her arms out to him. "I'm too dirty to hold you, little one," he protested, but Gemma slid the child into his embrace anyway. "I need to get something from her room upstairs," she said, making the excuse on the spur of the moment. "I'll be right back."

As she climbed the stairs, she could hear Jake talking to Sophie. Tears filled her eyes at the depth of tenderness in his voice as he showed off his work.

"This is what I did this morning. I'm not a carpenter, but I can do odd jobs. Mostly though I just tell the other people what we need done and they do it." Sophie babbled something and he laughed. "Yeah, Uncle Jake is lots better with plants than he is with building. I've got a ton of lovely plants coming. You can watch me plant them. Do you think your mommy will like this room? It's special because it's your mama's quilting room."

Upstairs Gemma paused inside the kids' room.

Jake would have been a wonderful father. She could imagine him cuddling his newborn, promising to ease his path, smiling with delight as his son reached a milestone. He would have been a fantastic husband, too. He was the kind of man who cherished a woman, the kind who gave her space to be herself but was there when she needed him.

Gemma gulped. How did she *know* these things about this man she'd met such a short time ago? Yet she was certain she had a handle on Jake's character. Why was that? Had she known him so well before? Again the desperation to remember settled on her heart. All the unexplained issues she struggled with—how much easier life would be if she could just remember her past life.

She recalled her talk with the aunties, how

they'd insisted that God was working in her life to make her more like His son.

"I don't know how my forgetting could make that happen," she whispered. "But I guess I need to trust You, don't I?"

With a weary sigh she rose, picked out three sleeper sets and returned downstairs. At the bottom she heard a faint hum. She stepped around the corner silently and froze at the tender scene.

Jake was perched against a sawhorse, rocking Sophie in his arms as he sang to her, telling her of God's love for children. It was a praise song Gemma faintly recalled. As she listened to the words, she marveled at the tenderness of his voice. Sophie's rapt gaze held his for the entire time. When he stopped singing, she reached up to brush his chin with her tiny fist.

Tears welled in Jake's eyes as he gazed at the child. Gemma stood frozen to the spot as moisture wet his cheeks and dripped off his agonized face.

"I miss you, Thomas," he whispered, his voice raw with emotion, eyes squeezed closed. "I'm sorry I failed you and your mom. I'm so sorry, son."

Gemma stepped back out of sight. This was a private moment Jake wouldn't want her to see. He was in a world of his own, a past he'd lost. Her heart ached for the pain he still suffered.

Why? she asked silently. *How could You be using such a loss for Jake's good? Can't You see how awful it is for him? Can't You help him?*

There were no answers. The same blankness that shielded her past also concealed whatever God was trying to tell her. It was so hard to trust when there was never any reassurance that answers would come. It must be doubly hard for Jake because he blamed himself.

Gemma so wished she could help him. Yes, she had plenty of money. She could buy a lot of things. But with deep clarity, she knew there was no *thing* that could help Jake.

Or her.

There was only trust.

God is our refuge and our strength. A tested help in times of trouble.

If ever there was a time of trouble, it was now. The aunties would say that the best, the only hiding place from all the doubts and worries that assailed her, was God.

"I will trust You," she whispered and marveled as a gentle peace quieted her heart.

"Gem? What's taking you so long?" Jake called.

"Trying to find a bag to put this stuff in," she said cheerily as she rounded the corner. "Guess Sophie's diaper bag will have to do."

There were few remaining traces of his emotional storm, but Gemma knew from the lines carved around his eyes that Jake's suffering continued. He'd merely shelved it for now.

God, please help Jake as he walks this lonely path.

Gemma prayed that over and over as she collected Alexa and Donnie and drove to The Haven. When she finally burst out laughing as the kids plastered themselves in paint after creating pictures for the renovated home, she was able to give Jake into God's care. Then, for the first time in ages, her heart felt light, happy.

It was only after she'd tucked the kids in, told them all another story about her overseas travels and was sitting on the back deck with the baby monitor, watching the stars come out, did she wonder why it seemed so imperative that she help Jake.

Of course he was her friend and she wanted happiness for him, but...

Only a friend? her brain wondered.

"I don't know if I can spend very long with you this morning, Alexa." Jake pointed out a weed that had taken root in her seedling flower garden. "Maybe just until Gemma gets back from her appointment."

Always Jake was concerned about getting too close, about letting his affection grow into something more. There was no permanence in life. He couldn't count on this child being here tomorrow and he didn't want Alexa to count on him. He was just a handyman.

Aren't you getting tired of pretending you don't want more? He ignored the query in his head.

"Gem's makin' a m'orial for Kurt," Alexa said. "What's a m'orial?"

"It's a time to remember someone," Jake explained.

"My mom din't gots one of those." Alexa looked sad. "She din't have nobody to do it. Our fam'ly was Mommy an' me, an' sometimes Kurt." She sniffed before digging into the earth with a firm shove of her tiny spade.

"I'm sorry. That must have been hard for

you. But you have lots of good things to remember about your mom." Jake smiled, hoping she'd talk about her memories because so far Alexa had not often spoken about her mother and he had a hunch that she needed to.

"Mommy loved God. Kurt helped her know how. He tol' us lots 'bout Him an' said we gotta never forget God loves us. No matter what." The child peered across the valley at the distant Rockies.

"Hey, you two. How's the gardening?" Gemma's cheerful voice startled Jake out of his musing. "You're not working very hard."

"We're talkin' 'bout m'orials," Alexa explained. "I'm m'orialing my mommy."

"That's nice." Gemma shared a look with Jake, but he couldn't translate the unasked question in her green eyes.

"Where are Sophie and Donnie?" Jake asked.

"With the aunts. Just for a minute. I need to ask Alexa something." Gemma squatted so she was at eye -level with Alexa. "Would you like to have a memorial for your mom at the same time as Kurt's? You could tell us about all the wonderful things you remember about both of them."

"Really?" Excitement chased away Alexa's sadness. "I could say 'bout how she always made water-lemon 'sert on hot days."

"You mean watermelon dessert," Gemma corrected.

"S'what I said." Alexa glared at her, then shrugged. "An' I could say 'bout how Mommy liked red. An' how I miss her."

"You could do all of that and we could share your memories. That's the best way to remember people who can't be with us anymore." Gemma glanced at Jake before adding, "I'd love to hear your memories about Kurt, too."

"'Kay. I'll do it." Alexa picked up an earthworm, studied it, then plopped it back on the ground and buried it. "When's it gonna be?"

"Not till after we finish Nancy's house," Jake said quickly.

"'Kay. I'm goin' to see Donnie now." Alexa skipped toward the house.

"I'm a little stressed," Jake confided. "We only have a couple of days left before Nancy and Jeremy come home."

"You'll get it all done." Gemma's smile warmed a part deep inside him that had stayed safely hidden for a long time, a part that he'd forgotten existed. "If anyone can do it, you can, Jake."

"I hope I live up to your faith in me." He felt totally inadequate, though he desperately wanted to prove her right. That was the Gemma-effect. She made people want to be better. She personified the love of God that the aunts spoke about.

Jake could almost believe in that love, except for his family. The kind of love that had taken them was something he couldn't comprehend. Maybe he never would.

"If I'm going to finish at Nancy's, I need

to get to work." He rose with a sigh as he realized that while he'd been with Alexa, the black guilt cloud had lifted. All he'd felt was love. He smiled as the little girl raced Donnie to where they were. He patted her head, enjoying her cute smile. "Bye, sweetie. Bye, Donnie."

"Donnie don't feel like talking t'day," Alexa explained. "An' he jus' eated a worm."

"Ew." Jake rolled his eyes until she giggled. "See you later?" he asked Gemma.

"After preschool. We're coming to hang the kids' pictures, remember?" She cocked an eyebrow at him. "The bedrooms *are* ready, aren't they?"

"Did you doubt my promise that they would be?" he snipped, liking the way her cheeks colored. "The bedrooms are re-floored, re-windowed and freshly painted. They're ready."

"Then what's wrong? Not the quilting room?" Worry darkened her gaze. That room was Gemma's personal project and she'd gone to great lengths to ensure it would be exactly what Nancy would need.

"No. The *big deal*," he emphasized with a grin, using their code words, "will be delivered and installed today. It's the bathrooms that have me worried. The tiles are still missing."

"I'll be praying for you and them." Gemma's megawatt smile sent a flicker of warmth to his heart. "We're almost there, *Jakey*," she said and giggled at his grimace. "God's not going to let us fail now."

"From your lips," Jake murmured. He figured her prayers were probably a lot more effective than his.

Gemma's reassurance had kept him going when issues seemed certain to stall progress at Nancy's and derail their surprise. In fact Gemma seemed more like her old self every day, even without the return of her memory.

Jake's affection for her was growing, too. So much so that it was becoming difficult to imagine a day without Gemma's sweet smile and cheery encouragement.

Warning, his brain squealed.

Chapter Nine

"It's amazing." With tears rolling down her cheeks and her kids clinging to her, Nancy gave a huge smile that erased the strain and tension from her face. "How do I say thank you for all this?"

Gemma figured her reaction was worth everything they'd struggled with.

"Your thanks will be your enjoyment of your home." Jake grinned and pointed at Gemma. "But if I got the colors wrong or whatever, blame her. She's the decorator."

"Not decorator. I only suggested a few things," Gemma said, eager to deflect attention from her part in the renovation. "Jake's the one who got it done."

"Thank you both. There isn't one thing I'd change." Nancy hugged The Haven's handyman for what Gemma figured was about the fiftieth time, then said, "I don't know where the funds to do this came from. Or those that paid for our trip for Jeremy's surgery. Or for the gorgeous trees and flowers planted all around the place. Amazing." She began listing all the changes but then shook her head when there were too many. "I wish I knew who's paying for everything so I could say a proper thank you."

"Enjoy your home," Jake said. "That's all the thanks anyone wants. That and seeing Jeremy get the care he needs."

"His prognosis couldn't be better. He won't have to hold his hand over his mouth anymore." Again tears welled in Nancy's eyes. Baby Sophie pressed her face into her mother's neck as if to console her.

"That's what we need to thank God for."

Gemma stuffed down her desperation to know if she'd chosen appropriately for Nancy's quilt room.

"I know how you c'n thank people." Alexa, her hand firmly holding Donnie's, stood in front of Nancy.

"How, sweetie?" the woman asked with a smile.

"Make 'em a quilt. You got lotsa stuff to do that an' that big new machine." She gave Gemma a quick glance.

"Alexa, honey, quilts are expensive and they take a lot of work," Gemma explained, praying the child hadn't figured out she was responsible for ordering the longarm quilting machine, *the big deal* as Jake called it, that now sat in the quilting room.

"Alexa, you are a very smart cookie." Nancy hugged the child until she wiggled to be free. "It's an amazing machine and I can hardly wait to use it. Thank you for thinking of that."

"Welcome." Alexa pursed her lips. "Kurt

usta say God gived us stuff so we'd use it ta make other people happy."

"He was right. I can hardly wait to get some time in that quilting room and try out everything." Nancy's longing look was interrupted by Jeremy's plea for a snack.

"The kids have missed you and Jeremy." Gemma laid a hand on Alexa's shoulder. "We'll go now so you can spend some time together."

"Okay. But tomorrow I'm going to have a big party and everyone who had any part in fixing this house is invited. Can you spread the word, Jake?" Nancy asked, smiling when he nodded. "Thank you."

Moments later they left Nancy inspecting the new children's play set that had been installed in her backyard.

"It's a good day t'day," Alexa pronounced with a yawn.

"It certainly is." Gemma shared a smile with Jake after he'd buckled the little girl into her car seat and helped her plug in her earbuds. "You did amazing work," she murmured so Alexa couldn't hear. "Thank you."

"Gemma, it was completely my pleasure to partner with you in improving Nancy's home." Their gazes locked. His smile did funny things to her knees. Thankfully his phone rang and drew his attention. "What? Oh, no. Okay, thanks. I'll be there shortly."

He hung up. All the elation from Nancy's surprise had drained from his face, leaving it a pale mask.

"What's wrong?" she asked.

"We need to get back to The Haven." Once they were moving, Jake explained, the lines of strain around his eyes revealing his concern. "One of the kids wandered away from his group and now they can't find him. I should have been there," he said, eyes narrowed. "I'm taking too much time off from my job, getting too involved in other people's stuff. Your aunts should have called me on it a while ago."

"Jake, that's silly. Even if you were there,

you can't monitor every single visitor," Gemma protested. "Besides, you've always put The Haven and my foster aunts before everything, including yourself. Getting involved in other's people's stuff isn't wrong. It's a blessing to the community."

A muscle in his jaw flickered but he did not respond. She was glad Alexa was humming to her music so they could talk.

"What's really going on with you, Jake?"

"A reality check. What happens when I'm not around anymore, Gem?" he growled. "What happens when there's no one to help out these folks who keep calling me?"

"You're leaving?" she gasped. Suddenly the sun dimmed and her world seemed bleak.

"Not today, but sometime. Then what?"

"Do you think you're the only person God has in His arsenal of helpers?" Gemma demanded as a wave of relief rushed over her. *Jake's not leaving.* "He placed the community's needy folks on your heart. If you're not willing to help, don't you think He can find others who will step in and fill in the gap?"

"You think what I've been doing was directed by God?" He gave a half laugh. "I doubt that."

"Because?" she demanded.

"Because I never asked Him for help, never sought out His leading on who to help."

She studied him, working it out in her mind and blinking at her conclusion.

"You don't think God's with you at all, do you, Jake?" she asked, stunned by that. "You believe He totally abandoned you the day Lily and Thomas died."

"Didn't He?" he demanded, his anger visible.

"No, Jake, He didn't." Somehow Gemma had to make him see God in a new way. "First of all you can stop taking all the credit for their deaths. I know you didn't leave your loved ones behind knowing that carbon monoxide would kill them." She continued, ignoring his attempt to interject. "You knew that chimney had been a problem and you were going to fix it, but first you needed to secure your family's future with that delivery. Correct?"

Jake shrugged. He didn't disagree, though his expression clearly showed he didn't accept her rationalization.

"You couldn't have known they'd die, Jake. There was no way to know. That's the thing about carbon monoxide." She thought of something. "Did you have an alarm?"

"Yes. They said it never went off, that it may have been faulty." His eyes grew hard, cold.

"And that was also your fault?" Gemma guessed with a groan. "You were supposed to know that how?"

"I bought the thing, Gem," he said through clenched teeth.

"But…" She couldn't argue with that because she couldn't think of a way to offer him a new perspective. He'd been hanging on to his grief and blame for too long.

So she remained silent until they were almost at The Haven, her brain desperately sorting through each detail she knew, searching for something to hang on to, something to prove to Jake that he could not have done more. Something to prove he was innocent of his family's deaths.

Only there was nothing.

"Gem?" Alexa's tone said there was a question coming.

"Yes?"

"Who do I b'long to?" the little girl demanded. "This song says we all b'long to someone, but I don't. I don't b'long to nobody."

Before Gemma could respond, a deer skittered across the road in front of them. She thrust out a hand just as Jake slammed on the brakes. The force sent her hurtling forward in her seat. Her head collided with the dash. For a moment she saw stars.

And then Gemma was a child, in a room, *her* room. It was nighttime. There was a beautiful, sparkly light shining over her princess bed. A woman hugged her close.

"Sleep well, darling," she whispered. "Tomorrow we'll fly to Hawaii and you can play on the beach for as long as you like."

The lady smelled like the flowers the florist brought every Friday and set in pretty jars all over their house.

"Daddy and Mommy love you so much, pretty girl. Here's a kiss, sweet Gemma." A man's strong arms lifted her up and a scratchy face brushed her cheek. "Sleep well, darling girl. See you tomorrow."

"Don't go, Mommy. Daddy, don't go." But they were gone. Gemma was all alone.

Then, in a tidal wave of memories, it all came cascading back. Her uncle waking her up, saying that her parents had gone away, that he'd take care of her. Only he'd gone away, too. One of the servants said the police had made him go to jail, but Gemma thought he'd gone to wherever Mommy and Daddy were. She didn't know where that was. She only knew they'd left her behind.

She'd cried and cried until a grumpy lady took her away and made her stay with people she didn't know, people who didn't understand that she wanted her teddy and her own clothes and her special shoes that Daddy said made her a beautiful ballerina. She didn't belong with any of them. She belonged with Mommy and Daddy. Why didn't they come back? Didn't they want her anymore?

Gradually Gemma's brain realized a voice was calling her name, but she ignored it to focus on remembering. She'd gone to other foster houses, lots of them. But they weren't home. Some places seemed so awful she couldn't stay, so she'd run away. She remembered her social worker bawling her out for getting in trouble. She remembered coming to The Haven, to her foster aunties and her foster sisters and desperately hoping that perhaps here she could finally belong.

But she hadn't really belonged here either,

not until she met Kurt. He'd made everything okay. Dear, wonderful Kurt had soothed and comforted her battered spirit, made her feel safe. When she confided her feelings of not fitting in, of not belonging anywhere, he'd shown her—though it had taken weeks, months, even years—that she was a child of God, that she belonged to God.

That He loved her.

"Gemma?" A hand on her shoulder brought full awareness. Jake stood by her open truck door, his fingers around her wrist, taking her pulse. "Are you all right?"

"Yes." She shook her head, winced at the faint tenderness on her brow and then glanced around. "I'm fine. Where's Alexa?"

"We're at The Haven. Alexa's with Victoria and her children. She's okay. She's just worried about you." His face tightened. "I'm sorry I hit the brakes so hard that you got hurt."

"I'm not hurt." Gemma would think about it all later. For now she picked up her purse off the floor and slid out of his truck, enjoying the feel of his helping hand under her elbow. "Why are you wasting time with me? We need to go look for that little boy."

"They found him. He's fine. He was with Sweetie." Outrage filled Jake's face. "The dumb old cow cornered him in the barn and wouldn't let him out."

A bubble of laughter inched up from inside. Gemma smacked her hand over her mouth. It wasn't nice to laugh when Jake was so serious, but she couldn't help it. She pulled her hand away and let her laughter spill out. It felt so good, as if all the worries and fears she hadn't been able to answer for so long now floated free.

"Uh—Gemma? Are you hysterical?" That made her laugh even harder. Poor Jake looked so confused.

"No, but a c-cow caused all this fuss?" She waved a hand to indicate the number of people who were returning to their cars, obviously searchers who'd come to help.

"Yes." His brow lowered. "Sweetie's not getting any oats tonight, trust me."

"Oh, Jake, your face." His glare made Gemma laugh again. "If you could only see your f-face," she said, trying not to giggle.

Finally he managed a laconic grin, though his eyes still searched hers.

"Tell me," he said after several moments had passed.

"What do you mean?" She brushed back her hair and exhaled, feeling freer than she had for weeks.

"Something's different about you." Jake studied her for an instant more before his mouth split into a huge grin. "You remembered," he crowed.

She nodded, unable to conceal her delight.

"Everything, Gem?"

"I think so. More than I realized I knew. I did have parents, Jake. We lived in a big house. They were going to a party and they kissed me goodbye." She touched her cheek with her fingertips, almost able to feel her

parents' caresses once more. "They were killed that night, but I didn't know that. Everyone said they were gone. They talked about me being left behind, so that's what I thought had happened."

"That they'd deliberately left you behind," he murmured. He let his breath out between his teeth. "That explains a lot."

"Alexa's question was like a trigger. I always thought they'd abandoned me. Ever since they died I've been trying to figure out where I belong."

"Until Kurt," he said softly.

"Kurt offered me security," she agreed quietly, wondering if she should reveal her long-hidden secret. "I clung to him because with him I felt safe. And then the earthquake stole that sense of security and I couldn't find it. Still haven't," she mused sadly. "Still can't quite figure out where I belong."

"You belong here, at The Haven."

"Perhaps." She gave Jake a sad little smile. "At least I finally figured out why I've felt

alone for so long." Gemma closed her eyes and visualized the past. "They said my parents had gone, Jake. They never said *died*. They said gone. I was only four, around Alexa's age. I couldn't understand why the ones I loved so much, the ones I thought loved me, would go somewhere without me, why they'd leave me on my own and not come back."

"Oh, Gem." Jake's arms drew her close as tears rolled down her cheeks. "You didn't understand that they hadn't abandoned you."

"Eventually I did," she sniffed. "But by then those feelings of not belonging were deeply rooted. Maybe my brain knew that my parents hadn't abandoned me, but my heart couldn't accept it." It felt so good to relax in his arms and release the fears that had lain inside for so long.

"Loving Kurt helped you through that," he murmured as one hand smoothed her long hair down her back.

"Mm, more like he helped me shelve it,

stop worrying about my past and get on with my life," she answered. Dare she tell Jake the truth? Would he understand or would he feel she'd betrayed the man who'd loved her with his whole heart.

"He knew what you needed," Jake said as she regretfully drew away. "He loved you a lot."

"I know." Gemma exhaled then admitted, "The thing is, I'm not sure I loved him the same way."

Shocked and certain he'd misheard, Jake pulled back to get a glimpse of Gemma's face.

"What did you say?"

"You heard me right." She glanced around, saw a huge boulder nearby and pointed to it. "Can we sit down while we talk?" She needed some distance between them.

"Sure." He made sure she was comfortable before lifting one eyebrow. "Start with your memories."

Gemma remained silent for several moments, though her gaze never left him.

"My parents were wealthy. Aunt Tillie and Aunt Margaret told me my family history when I turned eighteen because that's when I got control of my trust fund. It's huge," she said, green eyes stretched wide. "It pays dividends directly into my bank. That's why I have so much money in my accounts. From dividends. Not because I save so well." She rolled her eyes. "Sometimes I am so dumb. I told myself a tour guide must make a lot of money. From what? Tips?" She snorted in disgust. "Call me clueless."

Gem, gorgeous, smart and funny Gemma was a wealthy heiress. Jake needed time to process that. For now he nodded encouragement for her to continue while he appreciated the way she tilted her head to one side and lifted the shiny strands off her slender neck.

"After the aunts explained, I read online that my uncle embezzled a lot of my parents' assets when he was settling their estates. He was my guardian until some accountants figured out what he was doing. Then he went to jail and I became part of the foster system."

"Your uncle didn't get your money?"

"Some of my parents' estate, sure." She shrugged. "My father had most of my inheritance locked up until I reached eighteen though. That's why the aunts chose to tell me on my graduation." Gemma's smile faded. "It rocked me, I can tell you. So much so that I begged them not to tell anyone else. I didn't want my world to change any more than it already was."

"Change?" He couldn't figure out what she meant.

"Yes, I didn't want to not belong again. Remember, I was finishing school and planning on going overseas. Kurt couldn't decide what he wanted to do. We were going to be separated. He wouldn't be there when I needed him. I was terrified that I was making a mistake by leaving." She huffed out a sigh. "So I asked the aunts to oversee the details of my inheritance."

"And you've never touched it?" Jake asked.

"Didn't have to. Dividends, remember?" She needed him to understand. "I think that I deliberately kept these details suppressed because I've been subconsciously angry that they left me behind."

"You were angry at your parents?" he said, brow furrowed in confusion.

"At them, God, the foster system, my uncle, Kurt. All the people who failed me." She bit her bottom lip. "Maybe that's why I never quite believed Kurt when he said he loved me," she whispered. "Inside I was scared he'd leave me, too. The aunts didn't like that I'd eloped or that I'd never told him about my money."

Jake struggled to understand what she was saying.

"And they thought Kurt should have told you about Alexa," he murmured. "So you were both keeping secrets."

"Yes." Gemma sighed. "It wasn't right, but not telling Kurt—that somehow allowed me to enjoy what security I had, to let myself relax and savor being loved for myself. I thought it would never end," she added very quietly. "I was stupid."

"So when you say you're not sure you loved Kurt as he loved you...?" He had to ask, had to know.

"Kurt was very special to me. And I did love him dearly. He was gentle and kind and he taught me so much."

"But?" Jake couldn't have stopped himself from saying that if he'd tried.

"Kurt gave and gave. He did everything he could to be the husband any woman would want. He always made me feel special, cherished, wanted. Most of the time I was certain that I belonged with Kurt." Gemma studied her hands, head downcast.

"Most of the time?" He caught his breath when she looked at him. Her lovely face was now ravaged with grief.

"He gave me so much. What did I give back? Nothing but friendship." She rubbed her wet cheeks with her palms. "It was all I had to give. I realize that now. And Kurt never once complained, never said he wanted more. He always seemed happy. But then I heard…"

Gemma's words died away. Jake tensed. He knew she was going through some traumatic event that had set off this whole chain of self-doubt. But he wouldn't ask, wouldn't probe. If she wanted to tell him, he'd listen. As a friend.

"I overheard him praying once," Gemma whispered. Her gaze was far off, in the past. "We were escorting a tour through France last year. Our hotel room was the most gorgeous room with Louis XIV décor and the loveliest balcony. I woke up and he was sitting out there, probably so he wouldn't disturb me. He had his Bible open but he wasn't reading." She gulped. "He was weeping, Jake. Weeping for me. Begging God to let me love him as much as he loved me. Asking God to heal me so we could have a real marriage."

She twisted her head, eyes brimming with tears, her sadness tearing at his gut. Jake wanted so badly to wrap his arms around her and draw her close, to ease the pain of that memory and her guilty feelings.

"I think that's why Kurt never told me about Alexa," she whispered. "He wasn't sure he could trust me enough to love her the way he did. Because I couldn't love him enough."

His brain told him not to do it, but Jake ignored the warning. He couldn't stop himself. He slid his hand over hers and drew her upward, straight into his arms. All he wanted was to comfort her, to soothe this tortured woman, to take some of her suffering so she could once more be the special person he knew she was. At least that's what he told himself.

"I don't believe you didn't love Kurt,

Gem," he murmured, his cheek pressed against her lovely hair, his lips near her ear. "Maybe you didn't love him the way you thought you should, but I think you loved him just as much as you could. And I also believe Kurt knew that."

Gemma leaned back to stare directly into his eyes.

"Do you really believe that, Jake?" she said, her lovely green eyes dimmed. "Or are you only saying it to make me feel better."

"*I* believe it," he said firmly. "The question is, do you?"

Chapter Ten

On the day of Kurt's memorial, Gemma rose before dawn. She took her cup of coffee to the deck and huddled under one of her aunts' afghans to watch the sunrise while her mind recalled the first day she'd met him.

I'm Kurt Andrews and I'm going to be your friend.

Snapshot after snapshot clicked through her brain, sometimes making her smile, sometimes making her weep until that last precious moment before he'd disappeared.

"Thank you for giving me such a wonderful friend, God," she whispered as the pale pink fingers of sun crept over the horizon.

"Gem?" Jake stood at the corner of the patio, an insulated cup cradled in one hand. He studied her, those compassionate blue eyes dark with concern. "What's wrong?"

"Nothing." She dashed away her tears and managed a smile. "Just remembering Kurt."

"If it's going to be too much for you, you don't have to give the eulogy. I could do it for you," he offered quietly.

"Thank you, but no. I have to do it. I owe it to Kurt." She motioned to a chair, glad when Jake sat down. "It's the least I can do for him."

"You know Kurt would never say or think that. He wasn't much into accolades." A smile hovered over Jake's lips. "He once told me there were far too many people all taking credit for the same thing."

She nodded. "That was Kurt."

"What will you say, Gem?" Jake asked, his voice very quiet.

"That's why I came out here to think. I'm not sure exactly what I should say." She looked at him as her thoughts gelled. "Kurt liked to laugh. He loved God and he made a point of sharing his faith. That's the man I'm going to talk about. He wouldn't want a maudlin service. He always told me he was allergic to tears."

"You'll do great." Jake said it with such deep intensity that she got caught up in examining his handsome face. He looked tense, she realized, as if he was struggling with some inner demon.

Understanding dawned.

"You don't have to be there today, Jake." She touched his hand, trying to transmit her empathy. "Not if it will bring painful reminders of Lily and Thomas and their funerals. There's no reason for you to relive that."

Jake squeezed her hand but quickly released it. His shoulders went back. His chin lifted and he looked directly at her. "How do you do that?"

"Do what?" Gemma frowned at him in confusion.

"Worry about me when you've got your own emotions to deal with on this of all days?" A hint of anger underlaid his words. "It's I who should be comforting you, Gem."

"There's no *should* about today," she contradicted. "We've all lost a very good man. Whatever we can do to help each other deal with that loss is what we'll do." She paused before asking, "May I tell you something?"

"Of course. We're friends," Jake murmured.

"A year after I first came to The Haven, one of my schoolmates died tragically. I had a horrible time dealing with it. It reminded me of losing my parents, I guess. Anyway, I kept bugging Kurt about how I felt it was so terrible and how she'd had such big dreams and she'd never get to fulfill any of them. He listened to me babble about it for a week.

And then one day he sat me down and said, 'Look, kid, accept it. None of us know how long we're here for.'"

"Okay." Jake's dark eyebrows rose in an unspoken question.

"He'd always quote James 4:14. Do you know it?"

"Not offhand. What's it say?" Jake asked.

"'Ye know not what shall be on the morrow.'" Gemma smiled at the memory. "Kurt said that was his life's verse. I didn't understand it until he told me that he needed that reminder daily because nobody knew how long he'd have to make a difference in the world. He said that every day he got out of bed he needed to do whatever he could to make a difference. To me that sums up Kurt."

"I'm not sure exactly why you told me this."

"Because, Jake, if coming to his memorial upsets you or reminds you of how you lost your family, you shouldn't come," Gemma explained. "In fact doing so goes against everything he stood for. Kurt was about life, not death."

Jake stayed a few moments longer before he made some excuse about jobs he needed to do before the memorial. Watching him stride away saddened Gemma. When would he let go of his past? When would he stop blaming himself?

"Please show me how to help him," she prayed. "And give me strength today so I can encourage others."

Then she went inside to prepare.

Since talking to Gemma this morning, Jake had vacillated between attending Kurt's memorial and staying at The Haven. It wasn't just the memories such a sad occasion roused. It was also worry that his presence would divert Gemma's focus. His heart told him to be there for her, comfort her. His brain said to stand back, let her deal with this with her own strength.

He finally temporized by slipping into the church after everyone else was there. From his position in the corner he could still see Gemma, but he doubted she'd notice him.

A huge picture of Kurt, surrounded by dense jungle vegetation, Panama hat in hand, and grinning his trademark smile, took center stage. Pure white lilies in a tall vase stood in front. Jake gulped. He'd ordered lilies for Lily's funeral. Lilies and roses.

There was no picture of Anna, but her name was printed on a huge board next to Kurt's picture. A massive vase of lilies guarded it, too. Memories of the man he'd known, a man who'd dedicated himself to caring for Anna and Alexa and Gemma swamped Jake until he suddenly realized the organ music had stopped.

Gemma rose and walked to the podium.

"Welcome," she said, her voice rough. She cleared her throat and began again. "Kurt Andrews didn't like accolades, attention or applause. What he loved was showing off the world his Father, God, had created. That's why I chose this picture. Kurt was never happier than when he could share his appreciation of God's handiwork."

Gemma paused, seeming to struggle with her throat. Jake mentally cheered her on.

You can do it, Gem.

"Two months ago today Kurt's earthly life ended with an earthquake in an Incan citadel in the Peruvian Andes. I believe he's now appreciating God's creation in a whole new way."

Soft chuckles echoed around the sanctuary.

"As I told someone this morning," Gemma's eyes found Jake and stayed on him. "Kurt's mission in life was to make a difference every single day of his life. For as long as I knew him, he did that. And the world is better off for him having been part of it."

Come on, Gem, Jake said internally when she faltered.

"Perhaps the best way we who loved Kurt

can show our love is to pass on his legacy of making a difference in our world. Our actions affect others."

Only then did Jake notice that Gemma used no notes. She spoke directly from the heart, her voice firm yet tender.

"Kurt was many things to me. Friend, spiritual leader, companion, husband. I've been realizing lately exactly how much he brought to my world. He made it so much better. A very long time ago, when I first arrived at The Haven, Kurt taught me a song. It's called 'Brighten the Corner Where You Are,'" she told them. "And its words are as relevant today as they were when it was first published in 1913. They were words Kurt Andrews lived by. Let us honor Kurt's life by brightening our corner of God's world."

Jake wanted to applaud, but Gemma wasn't finished.

"Now I'd like to invite Alexa, Kurt's stepdaughter, to talk about him and her mom, Anna, who died tragically on the same day as Kurt. Alexa, honey?" Gemma remained in place, smiling encouragement as the little girl joined her.

"I'm scared, Gem," she whispered loudly, her fingers reaching for Gemma's.

"You don't have to be scared. We all loved Kurt. Didn't you?" Alexa's head tipped up and down in a strong nod. "Tell us about him and your mom. I'll be right here."

Alexa took her time, but finally heaved a huge sigh and smoothed out her pretty blue dress, which Jake knew Kurt had bought for her. Then she began.

"Kurt was my for-real dad," she said, her voice clear, not requiring any amplification by microphone. "He wasn't my borned dad, but Mommy said Kurt was better 'cause he choosed me to be his kid. My mom was going to uni—school," she substituted after stumbling over the word. Chuckles again filled the room. "Mommy din't have no money and she coun't 'ford to have me. She said Kurt got them married 'cause he wanted to help us. He helped lots. He teached me how to walk, an' how to read the picture cards he sended me, an' how to print in my special book."

Jake had never been more proud than he was now of this sweet child, as if she was somehow his to be proud of.

"Kurt buyed me lots of stuff, but I din't love him 'cause of that," Alexa said emphatically, as if daring anyone to argue. "I loved Kurt 'cause he loved me. He tole me that's how we're s'posed to love, like God does. Kurt tole me 'bout God an' how He loved us, even if sometimes we get bad. He learned me how to pray. Mommy said Kurt knew lots 'bout God. She readed me stories from the Bible he gived her. She tole me God was our bestest friend. Me an' Kurt an' Mommy always had lotsa fun." She gulped. "Kurt liked to laugh. It was loud, an' when I was little, sometimes it scared me. But then he'd hug me an' it would be okay."

Alexa stopped suddenly. Her head bowed.

Everyone could hear her soft sobbing. Jake ached to race to the front, lift her into his arms and comfort her. But sweet Gemma already had a hand on the girl's shoulder and was whispering something. When Alexa lifted her head, Jake saw her face was wet, but her blue eyes shone with love.

"When Kurt laughed—" The little girl giggled through her tears. "Mommy did, too. So did I. Everybody did. He was the bestest dad." She turned to Gemma. "C'n I tell them all 'bout Mommy, too?"

"Go ahead, sweetie." Gemma's encouraging smile made Alexa grin.

"My mommy was so pretty. She had long brown hair, not long as Gemma's but pretty long," she said. "An' she liked water-lemon. She liked it lots."

Jake smiled at the smothered laughter. How could you not love this sweet child?

"Mommy liked ta sing. She had a pretty voice, kinda like a bird. Sometimes Kurt'd sing with her." Alexa shook her head, eyes twinkling. "That wasn't so nice 'cause Kurt didn't sing good. Mommy said it was like hearin' a crow. She tole me I should sing louder to cover up his singin'."

This precious child had the entire room enthralled.

"My mommy tole me 'bout Gemma. She said Kurt loved Gem very much. That's why Mommy got 'vorced. She said Kurt'd always be my daddy, but he'd helped us 'nuff and now he had ta marry Gem. Mommy tole me that I had ta share Kurt's heart with Gemma. I din't wanna at first," Alexa admitted honestly. "But Kurt tole me he had 'nuff love to go around, for me an' for Mommy an' for Gem. He said I'd love Gem an' he was zackly right."

Alexa stopped. She seemed to suddenly realize that everyone was looking at her. Her face crumpled and she began crying.

"I miss Mommy an' Kurt," she bawled.

Immediately Gemma scooped her up into her arms and held her close.

"We all do, darling," she said, her voice wobbling over the words. She squeezed her eyes closed and then reopened them to focus on the audience. "My aunts, Tillie and Margaret Spenser, will now read God's promises to us."

Carrying Alexa, Gemma returned to her seat, her red-gold head bent. She cuddled the little girl close as the aunts softly read the thirteenth chapter of I Corinthians, the love chapter. It seemed to Jake no scripture was better suited to the man he'd known as Kurt.

Ten minutes later, after several people in the audience had also shared their memories of Kurt, the pastor reminded everyone of the luncheon in the church hall, pronounced a blessing and thanked everyone for attending the memorials.

Jake rose to his feet, suddenly aware that since he'd seen the lilies, he hadn't thought of Lily and Thomas once. His whole focus had been on Gemma and Alexa, and their loss.

All he wanted to do now was make sure

they were okay, but since it seemed everyone wanted to talk to them, he stayed in the background, serving coffee where needed and chatting with folks he knew while his gaze constantly returned to the slim, auburn-haired woman and the blonde child at her side.

In that moment Jake knew he'd do anything for them.

"It was a great tribute, Gem." That evening Jake sat across from her on the patio, no longer wearing his serious blue suit, but clad now in his familiar jeans, T-shirt and cowboy boots. "You and Alexa both did very well."

"Thank you." Gemma sipped her well-creamed coffee and let the strain roll away. "I'm not sure I said everything that should have been said. I probably needed notes. But I guess it's too late to fuss about that now."

"Alexa says you're having two headstones set in the local cemetery, one for her mother and one for Kurt." Jake's voice warmed her, though the evening wasn't chilly. "That was kind of you."

"Celia said there's no chance of recovering Kurt's body," she murmured. "I don't know about Anna, but I wanted a place where Alexa would be able to come to and think about both of them. And I wanted something to mark Kurt's life. I only wish we had pictures for Alexa. She worries she'll forget her mom."

"Why not contact her social worker?" Jake suggested. "Social services must have done something with Alexa and Anna's belongings, especially the personal stuff."

"How did you get to be so smart about this?" she teased. "And why didn't I think of it?"

"Well, you do have a lot on your plate, although..." He paused meaningfully.

"If you're going to say you're smarter than me, don't," she warned. "Am I not the one who solved Mr. Marten's housing situation and Mrs. Janzen's income shortage at the same time?"

"Yes, you are," Jake agreed with a grin. "I can't fathom where you got the idea that the woman should run a boarding house for senior men, but it certainly has worked out for everyone involved."

"Just a part of my brilliance," she snickered. "Wait! There's more to come."

"That's what I'm afraid of." Jake's droll expression made her chuckle. "Gem, you do understand that my expertise is plants and not renovating houses?"

"Oh, fiddle. You are a handyman, aren't you? And Mrs. Janzen's place only needed a few handy things done." How she enjoyed this repartee with him. "Ever think your problem is maybe you're too old to be doing such hard work, Jake?"

"Too old?" He glared at her, pretended to rise and then flopped back into his chair. "Oh, my back," he groaned in pseudo pain. "You could be right. Lugging those ancient iron bed frames down two flights of stairs nearly killed me."

"Poor baby. You need a good woman to look after you." Aghast at what she'd said, Gemma gulped. "Ah—"

"Are you offering?" Jake asked, with one dark brow arched.

Relief whooshed out of her. Surely it was a good sign that he could joke?

"Actually, I'm going to suggest you move into Mrs. Janzen's place." She couldn't help giggling at his outraged expression. "Why not? She'll feed you three square meals a day, do your laundry and get the other men to chat with you. She still has a vacant room on the bottom floor you could rent. No stairs. Sounds perfect."

"She takes seniors," he reminded, eyes rolling with disgust. "Which I am not."

"Then I guess you won't be whining when I tell you about my idea to fix the preschool's bathroom problems?" Gemma hadn't felt this carefree in eons. Was that because Kurt's memorial was over?

Jake studied her as silence yawned between them. Gemma was about to speak but he beat her to it, his voice quietly droll.

"I don't believe I fully understood the meaning of the word *minx* before today."

"Now you like it?" she asked, tongue-in-cheek. There were too many shadows to allow her to read his expression.

"I *like* you."

Had he really said that, or had she imagined it? And if he had, what exactly did he mean and what was she supposed to do about it?

"I like you, too," she responded. *Liked him too much?*

"Are you really okay, Gem?" Jake's gentle question reminded her of the tender way he'd held her that day at the soccer field, after she'd remembered the earthquake, when she'd bawled all over his shoulder.

Gemma cherished that sweet memory,

though his comment still lurked in the back of her brain.

You loved Kurt as much as you could. I think he knew that.

Gemma hoped, no, prayed, that was true. But she wasn't certain and that nagged at her. Kurt had loved her so much. Had she shortchanged him?

"What I'm really asking is if you're struggling with Kurt's death, with letting him go?" Jake's rich blue gaze seemed to penetrate through to her thoughts.

"No. That day at Machu Picchu is pretty hard to deny. I saw him die." She managed to smile, suddenly weary of explaining. "He's gone to a better place. That's settled in my mind."

"Then?" Jake looked at her expectantly.

"Just a lot of *I wish* going on at the moment." She dragged her fingers through her hair, trying to shake off the jumbling emotions. "I wish I'd appreciated him more. I wish I'd told him how much his friendship meant to me when I first came here and after."

"You did. I heard you say it often," Jake assured her.

"Maybe. But—"

"Don't go there, Gem," he said gruffly. "Believe me, I know going over and over it in your head doesn't do anyone any good. Rest in the knowledge that he loved you and knew you loved him. Remember the happy times you shared."

"Is that what you do, Jake?" The question slipped out. She bit her tongue, worried she'd hurt him by probing his pain.

"There were happy times." He exhaled heavily. "Thinking about them reminds me of what I've lost. So I try to forget."

"But that's wrong!" She was aghast. "Lily and Thomas are part of you, who you were, who you've become. You can't just stuff them away in some forgotten corner of your brain. That doesn't honor their memories."

"I don't want—"

"To remember? I know," she said gently. "But I'm pretty sure that in remembering lies healing." He didn't want to talk about them, but she pressed him anyway. "Tell me about Lily. What was her favorite color?"

"Pink." The response came automatically. "She always wore something pink. It suited her dark hair and dark brown eyes. She wasn't very tall, only up to my shoulder, but she was beautiful inside and out."

Jake was actually talking about Lily! Gemma could hardly believe it. Because she wanted him to continue, she asked another question.

"And Thomas? Did he take after you or his mother?"

"Both of us." A tender smile curved his lips as he stared into some distant place. "He never cried much, only when he was hungry. Or if he was cold. That kid hated being cold. He had dark hair, curly like Lily's, but my blue eyes. At least we thought they'd stay blue." Jake's voice broke off. He gulped and clenched his hands together, maybe to force down the pain. "I'll never know," he whispered.

"You can't forget him, Jake. Ever," she whispered.

"As if." He cleared his throat, only speaking when he'd finally regained his equanimity. "But remembering is too painful. It's better to suppress it all."

"Is it?" Gemma shook her head. "I think it only hurts more. Talking about Kurt, about what he liked, who he was, it soothes the ache of his loss."

"It's not the same," Jake snapped.

"You think not?" Gemma wouldn't push it because she wanted Jake to ponder what she'd said, not work even harder to keep his grief inside.

"Can we talk about something else?" Jake asked, a certain desperation underlying his voice.

"Sure. Let's talk about Billy and Ethel."

She lifted her hand to hide her smile. She'd shocked him. Good.

"What about them?" Jake uttered the words hesitantly, as if he was afraid of what he'd hear.

"I stopped by Billy's the other day to drop off a pie Adele had made for him. Ethel was there, and they were not arguing. They were laughing."

"Good." Jake's eyebrows rose as his eyes stretched wide. "So?"

"I think we should play matchmaker." Gemma was sure she couldn't have surprised him more.

"Uh, our projects have always been about meeting needs." Jake blinked.

"No difference with this one," she assured him.

"What needs would our matchmaking meet?" *Dubious* didn't begin to convey the skepticism in those blue eyes.

"Companionship, affection, friendship, camaraderie."

"And love." He frowned at her. "That's your ultimate goal, isn't it?"

"Not exactly a goal." Gemma deliberately chuckled as if he'd said the funniest thing in the world, instead of hitting the nail on the head. "If they fall in love, that's their business. I just want to make it easier for them to be together."

"Why?" Suspicion lurked in that one word.

"I recently learned that Esther has hated living alone since her husband passed. She stays in that big old house of his family's, even though it's depleting her resources, because she believes she's doing her duty to the family."

"How *do* you find out these things, Gem?" Jake shook his head. "Guess I should be glad you're not suggesting we renovate it."

"Are you kidding? It must be over four thousand square feet on those three levels." Gemma shook her head. "Billy's place would be perfect for them both."

"Billy's place was also Irma's place," he reminded.

"That's where you and I come in." Jake's aggrieved expression sent Gemma into peals of laughter. "It's nothing bad. I just think we should help Billy sort through Irma's hundred million knickknacks. Not to get rid of, but perhaps to *bequeath* to his daughter or daughter-in-law."

"I have no words to describe the conniving brain tucked under your mass of beautiful hair," Jake murmured after several moments had passed.

"I'm not conniving." Gemma didn't like that he might think that of her. "I want to help. We both know Billy's very lonely. And Aunt Margaret isn't interested in him."

"Huh?" Jake sat in rapt attention as she related Aunt Tillie's confidence about Billy's crush on her sister.

"See? We'd be helping him get over that. Besides, lately Billy and Ethel seem to have plenty to talk about. And she loves cooking for him."

"Not that prune-pie thing?" he asked in disgust.

"Try prime rib with Yorkshire pudding. Peking duck. Southern-fried double-dipped chicken." She watched Jake's lips curve into an O-shape of surprise. "Those are only three of eighteen recipes Ethel got from Adele."

The Haven's handyman appeared completely taken aback. When he finally spoke, his voice brimmed with awe.

"What do you want to do?" he asked meekly.

"Put the health authorities on him." Gemma held up a hand to stop his protest. "I mean, *pretend* to do that."

"How?"

"By spreading a rumor that they're coming to investigate. You saw how Billy reacted when he suspected Ethel would summon them. He was afraid and he let us dust." She frowned. "I don't think he enjoys the mess his house is in now, but I believe even thinking about changing it overwhelms him. Perhaps the threat of the health department is the one thing that would force Billy to act, especially if we generously offer to help him get the place sorted *before* authorities can show up."

"You are a very devious woman." Respect echoed in those words.

"No, I just want to help Billy and Ethel. This happens to be the only plan I can come up with to achieve that. Well?" she demanded when Jake kept gaping at her. "Say something."

"Do you know what I appreciate about you, Gem?"

"Huh?" She frowned, not following.

"Actually there's a lot. First, you don't mind going into an old man's dusty, dirty place, where no woman has lived for eons, and helping clean it up so he'll have a second chance at love. Your temerity-slash-compassion is awesome." He pretended to clap.

"Oh, stop it." She blushed.

"Of course there's the little issue of lying. I should tell your aunts on you," he warned.

"It wouldn't be a lie. It'd be—a rumor," she substituted.

"Also, what if all that mess and dirt is what attracts Ethel? You never know. Maybe Billy's magnetism for her is that she'll get to make that place sparkle."

"I can't imagine—oh, you're joking." She heaved a sigh of relief. "So what are you saying? Will you help me?"

"How could I refuse?" He rose. "As it happens I'm going over there now. The church ladies asked me to take him a box of leftovers from the luncheon after Kurt's memorial. Want to come? We could drop your, er, hint about the health department."

"Isn't it too late to visit?" she asked, glancing at her watch.

"Not for Billy. He stays up for the really

late, late news." Jake glanced around. "I haven't seen Alexa this evening."

"She went to bed early. She was worn out." Gemma stood. "Can you wait while I ask Victoria to listen for her?"

"Yep."

She felt his eyes track her until she was inside The Haven.

"Going somewhere?" Victoria asked from her perch by the kitchen table.

Gemma quickly explained their errand, though she said nothing else. Victoria's eyes glowed with a knowing look, but she merely nodded.

"Don't be too late," she said in a motherly way. "Kurt's memorial took a toll on you, Gem, even though you might not feel it yet."

As she sat in Jake's truck on the way to Billy's, Gemma assessed herself. She didn't feel worn or tired. She felt revitalized. Was that because she was with Jake or because they were on their way to trying to help someone else?

Whatever the reason, she felt like she was beginning a brand-new chapter of her life and that Kurt would have wanted that for her. Wouldn't he?

Chapter Eleven

With summer now in full swing and what Jake called their "Matchmaker" project underway, life at The Haven became busier than ever. As hordes of kids arrived to enjoy days, weekends, or a whole week of riding, hiking, singing, camping and learning about God, Gemma kept volunteering for extra jobs.

As if running herself ragged could ease her brain's unease about her growing attraction to Jake.

Most afternoons they worked with Ethel and Billy, sorting a lifetime of possessions into what was needed and what wasn't. To

Gemma's surprise, the threat of the health department became unnecessary after the couple asked for their assistance in clearing out Billy's home. They quite openly discussed their growing feelings for each other and their plans to eventually marry. Jake demanded to know what Gemma had put in their water.

Gemma also partnered with Jake on their preschool project and in spending time with Alexa, who loved being with Jake.

"I like our garden," she repeatedly proclaimed. "I 'specially like eatin' garden stuff."

She'd already helped pick beans several times and was vigilant about checking the pea plants, eager to pinch off the fat green pods and feast. But it was the flowers that gave Alexa the most joy.

Early this morning Gemma had suggested they take a bouquet to the graveyard to place by her mother's headstone.

"My mom would like these red ones,"

Alexa said as she laid them down. As she sat crouched on the grass, she touched the cold, hard stone and tears rolled down her face. "I can't hardly 'member Mommy no more."

That was the one worry Gemma couldn't fix. She'd repeatedly tried to connect with Alexa's social worker with no success. In her last call, she'd left a message suggesting a visit to The Haven might be in order in a desperate ploy to help the little girl.

Today, after breakfast, Alexa's social worker, Dana, had arrived. She'd spent most of the morning with Alexa who had acted as official tour guide at The Haven.

"I'm glad you came to check on her," Gemma murmured when they'd finished lunch and the little girl had raced off to water her flowers with Jake.

"Someone should have been here weeks ago," Dana apologized. "I was her original worker, but her case was given to someone else. She went off on maternity leave and

Alexa's case fell between the cracks before I was reassigned."

"There's no worry about her leaving here. We'd love to have Alexa stay with us for the entire summer," she told Dana. "We all love her." They both watched Alexa working beside Jake as they removed weeds from the carrot patch.

"She does seem happy here," Dana mused. "To tell you the truth, seeing her so at home with you and your family is a big relief. When I first had contact with her, she seemed so lost. I've been worrying that she'd feel like she didn't belong. Many kids who go through a sudden and tragic loss of a parent have a difficult time, but she seems remarkably well-adjusted."

"She's a generally happy child, though one thing keeps recurring in our conversations." Gemma leaned forward, sensing an opportunity. "Alexa is worried she's forgetting her mom. She doesn't have any pictures or personal effects. Can you help with that?"

"I know there were personal effects recovered from their apartment. Because I was in charge of her case then, I ordered everything to be placed in storage. Let me check if it's still there." Dana dialed a number and began asking questions.

More than twenty minutes passed while Gemma told herself not to appear anxious or worried. Still, a wave of relief swept over her when the call finally ended.

"I'm sorry that took so long. Apparently we still have everything in a short-term storage facility, but that will expire at the end of the month. Then everything is scheduled to be moved into something more long-term." Dana thought for a minute. "I could go through it all, if you like, see if I could find a picture of her mom. Would that help?"

"Yes." Gemma thought about it a moment longer before she asked, "Are there a lot of things? If not, maybe you could send the whole lot here. Then Alexa could go through everything herself. Perhaps that would twig old memories and maybe ease her mind." She had a hunch this was the right move. "I'll gladly pay for express shipping."

"That's very generous of you," Dana murmured.

"I believe it's very necessary. Before we held the memorial for my husband, Alexa mentioned her mom hadn't had a funeral or memorial or anything, so we included Anna in Kurt's service. Alexa loved sharing her special memories, but I think it also sparked more fears that she's forgetting something about her mom." She met Dana's gaze square on. "That's the last thing I want. No child should forget her mom, not when we can help her remember."

"You know, my superiors agreed to let Alexa come here because your sister is a well-respected foster parent, because of your aunts' reputations and because of your husband's relationship to the child." Dana looked thoughtful. "But I see now that you have the same quality as they, a focus on working for the child's benefit and not on how uncomfortable or complicated it makes your own life. Alexa is a very fortunate child."

"Actually, we're the fortunate ones." Gemma knew it was true.

"How so?"

"Alexa has made a big connection with Jake, our handyman. He's experienced great loss in his life. I believe Alexa's presence is helping him finally accept what happened." Gemma smiled. "She's also been very good for me. I can't mope or isolate myself. You don't get away with anything when Alexa's around. She says Kurt and her mom taught her about God's love and she continually reminds us of how blessed we are."

"That's sweet," Dana said, sounding distant.

"It's also true." Gemma chuckled. "Continually being reminded to take a heavenly perspective on our situations has made both Jake and me less prone to wallowing in our troubles. Because of Alexa, I'm more fo-

270 Rocky Mountain Memories

cused on community involvement. She helps us with that, too, and loves every minute of it."

"What kind of community involvement?" Dana wondered.

Gemma smiled at the memories of spending time with Jake.

"Delivering food hampers, working with folks who need small renovations to their homes, local projects assisting seniors, visitation." She shrugged. "Whatever's needed. Most of the time it's Jake who's doing the helping. I'm just the gofer."

"Sounds like a great way to enjoy time together." Dana's smile held speculation. "Are you two—together?"

"Jake and I have been friends since I first came to The Haven years ago." Gemma wasn't going to tell her that most evenings they met to discuss progress on their current undertaking and to decide which project to tackle next, or that *his* outreach had now become *their* partnership. It was at those times when Gemma was absolutely certain that this was where she belonged. "Alexa loves to be included. The seniors particularly love seeing her happy smile."

"Alexa has a very big heart," Dana agreed. "I'll check into that storage and find out if I'm allowed to send her things here."

"Thank you. My biggest concern is ensuring Alexa feels secure. That's why I believe that having some of her mom's things, *their* things, would really help her," Gemma murmured.

By the time Dana waved goodbye, apparently satisfied that Alexa was well cared for, it was midafternoon and Gemma had grown very thirsty. She glanced across the yard and smiled at what she saw. Wearing wide-brimmed hats to protect against the direct sun, Jake and Alexa were back in his garden. This time they were picking spinach.

Gemma walked to the kitchen, filled a thermos with iced tea and set it in a basket with three plastic glasses and a bowl of freshly cut watermelon chunks. She laid her new picnic quilt, a recent gift from Nancy, on top. Then she walked to a spot just inside the garden gate and laid out everything on the soft green grass.

"Come on, you two," she called. "Time to take a break."

"We're havin' a picnic!" Alexa, her hand firmly attached to Jake's, tugged him toward the blanket, a huge grin lighting up her sweet face. "I like picnics."

"Me, too. You do know the other kids are making ice-cream sundaes?" Gemma asked with a wink at Jake. "Don't you want to join them?"

"Nope." Alexa flopped down on one side of the blanket and speared a piece of watermelon. She popped it into her mouth and then tried to speak around it. "Me 'n' Jake," was all Gemma understood.

"Excuse me?" She could barely suppress her laughter as Alexa gulped down the juicy fruit and then repeated what she'd said.

"Me an' Jake think some of the other kids would like to plant flowers, like I did." Alexa popped another watermelon chunk into her mouth.

"Actually, I said I wonder if some of the kids who come here might like to garden, learn about where their food comes from." Jake shrugged. "Just an idea for next year."

"Who are you and what have you done with the aunties' handyman?" Gemma demanded, shooting him a cheeky grin. "You know. The guy who insisted my three foster sisters and I had to learn how to mow lawns and weed flower beds before we could even get near your precious garden."

Jake rolled his eyes.

"Tell me how it would work," she said. Here was another chance to collaborate.

"To begin with, if you'd get my shed emptied, we could use it as a potting shed," he grumbled, inclining his head toward the building where she'd stored everything that had arrived from her Toronto apartment.

"*Your* shed?" It suddenly felt like Jake was pushing her to deal with her past, though he couldn't possibly know much she'd been procrastinating. "There must be other spaces available."

"Not ones so near the garden. It's a perfect potting shed. You have to empty it sometime, Gem. You can't leave your stuff there until winter," he said calmly.

"Why can't I?" Truthfully, Gemma would prefer to leave it there forever. She'd barely begun to shed her insecurities about Kurt. Why resurrect them now?

"Because it will get damp and that will ruin any pictures or keepsakes you have," he shot back. "Besides, a pile of stuff like that encourages mice."

"Don't you like mouses?" Alexa asked, wide-eyed.

"This handyman does not allow mice in any of the buildings he cares for," Jake explained in a pseudo-stern tone.

Gemma was glad of the interruption and

of Jake's concentration on the child. It gave her a few precious moments to gather her composure. Hopefully he wouldn't realize how desperately she wanted to avoid digging through her past life.

"There's your friend David," she heard Jake say and glanced in the direction of his pointing finger. "I think he's needs a friend. Why don't you take him some of this watermelon, Alexa?"

"Okay." The little girl chose the treat and scampered away. She carefully opened the gate, let herself out and then refastened it. After she'd handed David a spear of watermelon, they began an animated conversation. Moments later David's counsellor appeared and Alexa called to say they were going with him to play soccer.

Gemma nodded and waved. "How did you remember that boy's name, Jake?"

"Before any new group arrives, Olivia texts me a file with their names and whatever personal details we know about their

situation. I try to memorize as much information as I can." Jake shrugged as if that
was a simple thing. "It helps me keep an eye
out to see if they need something."

"Wow!" She gaped at him, mentally doing
the math over how many children visited
The Haven. "More of your outreaches," she
said in wonder. Appreciation for his giving
heart welled inside her. "You're quite a guy,
Mr. Handyman."

"I'm an ordinary man who's very curious
as to why you're so reluctant to deal with
your stuff," he said, eyes narrowed. "You
had the movers stack the boxes in there and
then locked the door. To my knowledge you
haven't been back. What's with that?"

Gemma thought about prevaricating, but
she doubted he'd let her get away with it, so
she remained silent.

"Are you avoiding something, Gem?"
Yes!

"I'll help you go through things, if you
want." That was Jake. Always the giver. But

he never took, never asked her to share his solitary hikes. "What's the issue?"

"I don't want to see it," she muttered.

"See what?" Jake reached over and tipped up her chin so he could look into her eyes. "Spill it."

"Proof of how bad a wife I was." There. She'd said it aloud.

"Gemma, there is no way." His eyes, bright in his tanned face, chastised her. "You loved Kurt. I saw it myself. I think maybe since the accident your brain is playing tricks with your memory. Trust me, you did love him. You have nothing to be ashamed or afraid of." He broke off speaking to purse his lips. "It's I who failed in my marriage."

"Jake." She sighed. "I keep telling you you're not to blame—"

"Yes, I am. There were many occasions when I wasn't the husband Lily needed, or the father Thomas should have had." The self-loathing in his words was painful to hear. "Thomas was a sickly baby. It's no wonder Lily was terribly run-down. But I was so focused on my business, myself and *my* career. She had to beg me to help with his bath time sometimes, or to rock him to sleep. I was always busy. I missed so much..."

Jake's voice died. He twisted his head to peer at the Rockies in the distance.

"Why don't you count the many times you've helped me?" Gemma touched his fingers with her own and reminisced. "From the first day I came here you took pains to help me adjust. You listened to me whine when I couldn't fit in at school. You helped me understand how to be a friend and not just wait for someone to befriend me. You even helped smooth things over for me when Kurt and I came to announce we'd eloped and he argued with the aunts."

"I didn't do anything special," he mumbled.

"Yes, you did, Jake. When we left here, the tension there had been was eased, because of you. All these years, no matter how left out I felt, you'd always insist that I could belong, if I wanted to." She lowered her voice. "I don't think you did that for my foster sisters. It was me you focused on, ensuring I felt like an important part of the family. I can never thank you enough for all you did for me."

"I don't want thanks."

"I know." She sighed and released his hand, hating to let go but needing all her focus to say this. "I wish that somehow I could repay even a little of what you did for me. You're very special to me, Jake."

"Big brother." He smirked and arched an eyebrow.

"No." Gemma bent her head and studied her fingernails. "A man I'm coming to care for very deeply, more than I ever expected or imagined."

"What are you saying, Gem?"

His voice demanded that she look at him, so she did, and this time she let the turmoil of uncertainty and affection and confusion reveal itself in her expression.

"I think I had a crush on you back then,

Jake. I'm beginning to wonder if that's why I feel like I failed Kurt, why I couldn't be the wife he deserved." She gulped and forced out the rest. "I never thought of it like this before, never took the time to probe my brain and try to understand, I guess."

"Now you have?"

"I'm realizing that for me, Kurt was safe. The day he first rescued me at school, I told myself I belonged with him and I just kept repeating that. To question it, to even hint that I didn't—it made me feel so insecure. It scared me to death."

Silence hung between them. Jake stared at her as if she'd grown two heads, obviously stunned by what she'd said.

"Maybe the reason I didn't love Kurt enough was because I had a crush on you." She gulped before admitting, "Maybe I still do."

A thousand things spun through Jake's brain, all of them bad. He was deeply moved that Gemma had appreciated his help all those years ago, and even more touched by her belief that she could care for him. But she couldn't care. Not like that.

If she knew, if she understood how selfish he'd been, how often his total self-focus had come between him and Lily...

"Why don't you say something?" Gem murmured.

"If I helped you all that time ago, then I'm glad. But please don't let your accident or Kurt's death muddle the truth. You did love Kurt. With all your heart." He smiled, wishing he could avoid this. "Anything you think you feel for me—it's not love. You're just vulnerable right now."

Once he'd daydreamed about Gem loving him. Instead he'd witnessed her deep devotion to Kurt. Now she was alone, mourning and trying to figure out her future. He had to warn her off. Even if she did love him, which he doubted, he could do nothing about it.

Because of his vow.

"I'll always be your friend, Gem, and I'm

glad we can share things." What a tame way to describe his special moments with her. "But don't make it more than it was, then or now. Especially don't feel guilty about being my friend."

"It's become more than friendship, Jake." Gemma's voice was whisper soft.

"It can't be," he said simply. He hated saying it, hated watching pain fill her face. But there was no other way. "I'm not someone anyone can love, Gemma. I can't have love in my life because I ruin it. Lily loved me once with a precious, beautiful love, and I threw it away."

"But—"

He pressed his forefinger against her lips and shook his head.

"I was blessed when God gave me Lily and then Thomas. I said I loved them. But love doesn't let selfishness and work take over and ruin everything. I messed up. Badly." He withdrew his hand, too aware of the brush of her velvet-soft skin beneath his fingertips.

"Even if that was true, and it isn't, it doesn't mean you can't ever love again," she argued.

"Yes, Gemma," Jake said firmly. "It does."

"Why?" she demanded, tears rolling down her cheeks.

"Because the day I buried my wife, I made a vow that I would never again jeopardize another woman with my so-called love. My neglect cost Lily and Thomas their lives. Taking them is how God punished me."

"God doesn't do that," she whispered, her face ravaged by tears. "God doesn't kill the people we love for our mistakes. You're wrong."

"I will keep my promise, Gem. I'm sorry." Jake rose and walked away. He had to. It was either that or wrap Gemma in his arms and try to soothe the pain he'd caused. He wasn't going to do that because he couldn't bear to think of Gemma one day paying for his neglect.

But oh, how he wished he could accept that beautiful gift of love she'd offered him.

The problem was, to do that he'd have to accept that God had let his family die. Because of his mistakes.

That acceptance wasn't going to happen. Ever.

For the next few days, Gemma avoided Jake as much as possible. When she went with him to call on two of the townsfolk who needed help, she pretended everything was fine. She even maintained the friendship image Jake had spoken of. But privately she fought an inner battle of confusion. Did she love him? How could she prove it to herself? Or him?

By dealing with her past.

On Friday morning, while Jake was in town repairing someone's flooring, and Alexa was making doughnuts with Adele, Gemma unlocked the shed and began going through the things from her past life with Kurt. Unaware of the passage of time, she opened each box and let herself savor memories tied up in the contents. So many things she'd done for and with Kurt. Surely she'd loved him?

With no answers, she began sorting what could go and what she would keep.

"Whatcha doin'?" Alexa demanded.

"Sorting. Want to help?"

"Sure." Alexa tossed her apple core across the fence to Sweetie and then began placing piles of Kurt's clothing in the boxes Gemma indicated.

Gemma had thought she wanted to be alone to do this, but Alexa's presence was a comfort. Her barrage of questions and fulsome memories about the man they'd both cared for helped revive reminiscences of the joy she'd shared with Kurt.

"He sure liked bright colors, din't he?" Alexa held up a tie-dyed orange and purple T-shirt.

"I gave that to him when we were in India." Gemma laughed at Alexa's disgusted look. "He said he wanted a purple memory."

"Ew." The little girl stuffed the shirt in a box. "Did'ja buy these, too?" She held up a pair of frayed green shorts whose better days were long gone.

"No. His mom gave him those when we came home to tell them we were married. Kurt called them his wedding present." Gemma closed her eyes, remembering how delighted he'd been that his mother had sewn something specially for him.

"How come they gots funny legs." Alexa frowned.

"Kurt tried to patch them. He didn't sew as well as his mom." Alexa's expression made Gemma laugh so hard that she doubled over.

And so it went, item after item eliciting some fond memory of the man who'd played a big part in both their lives.

"C'n I keep this?" Alexa held up a thin silver chain. "Me an' Mommy gived it to Kurt for Christmas one time."

Touched by Alexa's memory, Gemma

nodded, smiling as the little girl tucked it in her pocket.

"C'n I have some pictures, too?"

"Tell you what. Miss Dana said they found the things they got from your house when your mommy died. She's going to send them here." Gemma smoothed Alexa's glossy hair. "When they come, you and I will go through them, add these pictures, and make a special album so you'll always be able to look at them and remember both your mom and Kurt. Okay?"

"'Kay. I gotta have more pictures though. 'Cause when I go 'way, I want to remember everybody at The Haven."

The overwhelming sadness in that thought hit Gemma hard.

Where would Alexa go? With whom would she live? Would they care about her past? Would they keep Kurt and Anna's memories alive?

"Do you like it here, Alexa?" Gemma couldn't promise anything, not with her own world so unsettled. But she did want to hear the child's feelings on being at The Haven. Was she happy?

"Yeah, I really like it." Alexa's voice wobbled. "The other kids only come for a little while, 'cept the ones that live here. I don't live here so I gotta go, too, I guess, but I dunno where."

She sounded so down about it that Gemma worked hard to make her giggle and smile as they went through the rest of the items.

"You gots lots of these picture books." Alexa flopped down on the ground and opened one. "You an' Kurt are always laughing."

"We laughed a lot. I always made a book when we went to a place we'd never been before." Gemma sat down beside her and let the memories cascade as she answered Alexa's questions.

When they'd gone through the last book, they packed them all in a box.

"Are you keeping all of this stuff?" Jake

asked, surprising them with his noiseless appearance.

"Hi." Gemma couldn't stop the bubble of delight from fizzing inside her. "No. Those boxes of clothes are going. So are the trinkets. These four boxes are personal things I'm keeping."

"She's got lotsa pictures." Alexa danced up and down. "Me an' Gemma are gonna make a book for me, too. An' you're gonna be in it."

"Really? I'm very honored, Miss Alexa." He ruffled her hair, shaggy now that it was growing out. When he glanced at Gemma, she caught her breath. "Was it as bad as you anticipated?"

"No." She smiled. "You were right. I needed to go through these. It's been...cathartic."

"Here's a place you went where there's snow houses," Alexa piped up, leafing through loose pictures. "Do you always gotta wear big boots in that place?"

Gemma burst out laughing at Alexa's offended expression, and to her surprise Jake joined her.

"That place is called the Arctic, Alexa," he said. "You need big boots to keep your feet warm."

"You knew I'd gone to the Arctic?" Surprise filled her that Jake knew of that trip.

"I saw all the postcards you sent the aunts, Gem. I always knew when you were on a trip." His low rumbled tone did funny things to the equilibrium she was trying so hard to maintain.

"Oh." She couldn't make herself look away from his gentle sky-blue eyes.

"Where are ya gonna send all Kurt's funny clothes?" Alexa's shrill voice broke the tension.

"Good question. I'll load what you don't want in my truck. We could donate or dispose of it. Your choice." Jake waited for Gemma's nod before carrying the boxes to his waiting truck with Alexa trailing by his side.

Gemma's phone rang. It was Victoria.

"Gemmie, we're stuck. Our presenter for tonight can't make it. Which is a pain. He's a puppeteer and the kids were really looking forward to seeing him. Can you step in for him?"

"I'm no puppeteer, Vic," she declined.

"No, but everyone loves your amazing stories about fantastic places all over the world. You have pictures, too. Couldn't you use them?" Victoria wheedled. "The kids will be on the edge of their seats."

Gemma recalled her month-long tour of Africa. The unique animals and people she'd discovered would certainly lend themselves to a kids' presentation.

"Okay," she agreed. "But if they all fall asleep or take off, it's on you."

"Not gonna happen, kiddo. Mega thanks. You'll do great."

"Who's that?" Jake asked, arms loaded

with boxes filled with her books. He grinned when she explained. "Then I guess you'll want one out of these," he said, glancing at the boxes of books.

"I have everything on my computer. I just need to put it together for a slideshow. If you could hang a sheet or something, I'd really appreciate it," she said with a glance around. "I'll store the stuff I'm keeping in my room."

"Okay." He set the chosen boxes in the back seat of his truck.

Gemma's heart thudded as they rubbed shoulders on the way to The Haven. Alexa had insisted on sitting by the door, leaving her squeezed next to Jake. Once they arrived, Alexa lost interest in things and went to find her friend David.

Gemma followed Jake inside the house, carrying the diary she'd kept since she'd been married and her laptop. "At least if I mess this up tonight I can still go back to touring," she muttered as they climbed the stairs.

Jake paused at the top, his face alert. "You're thinking of doing that?"

"Maybe. My company called. They've had requests for me to do a small group, in-depth tour of Egypt," she explained.

"Egypt was always your favorite, wasn't it? I remember you took a lot of history courses about it." Jake set the boxes on the floor.

"The pharaohs, the pyramids, the Nile— it fascinates me." She shrugged. "I'd love to go back. But—"

"But?" He paused, studied her. "But what?"

"I'm not quite sure touring is where I belong," she told him as her brain silently begged, *Tell me not to go, Jake.*

"You'd do an amazing job," was all he said before he left to retrieve more boxes.

"Thank you," she mumbled, wishing he'd ask her to stay.

When everything she wanted was in her room, Jake led the way back downstairs where Alexa sat moping at the table because

David had gone on a hike without her. Jake chucked the little girl under the chin.

"You've got more blooms on your flower-pot flowers, missy. Want to go check them out?"

"Yes! Are they giant flowers like the pictures showed?" Alexa was halfway out the door, dragging Jake with her, when she stopped and turned. "C'mon, Gem. We gotta see my flowers."

"Right behind you." Gemma rose. She'd put her slideshow together after supper. She knew exactly the Biblical story to go with it.

When they arrived at Alexa's plant pots, the little girl looked downcast.

"What's wrong, kiddo?" Jake asked, squatting beside her.

"They're dinky flowers." Alexa glared at the blooms.

"They've only just begun to bloom," he told her as she leaned against him. "Give them time."

"They've had to work very hard to bloom,

honey," Gemma added, searching for a way to make her words reach Jake, too. "We're nearly in the mountains. It's not the kind of home these flowers are used to so they have to adapt."

"What's 'dapt?" Alexa asked.

"Well, it means that it's not as warm here as where they usually grow, and that we get cooler nights, and maybe the soil isn't as good as it is in other places." Gemma risked a glance at Jake. "These flowers have to find a way to deal with all of that. But even though they have to struggle, they are still beautiful."

"Why doesn't God make 'em grow bigger?" she demanded.

"How do you know He isn't?" Gemma held Jake's gaze. "God promised He'd always be with us, no matter what happens."

"Was He with you when the earth—when Kurt died?" Alexa asked, her face thoughtful.

"Yes, honey. Just like He was with you

when your mom died. God's always with us." Gemma bit her lip as Jake rose, his face set.

"I've got chores," he said stiffly before striding away.

"Jake's sad," the little girl said with a sigh. "I singed to him yesterday and I tol' him some jokes, too, an' he's still sad. I dunno know how to make him not sad."

"Sometimes people can't do that, even though they really want to." Wasn't that the truth?

"How come?" Alexa demanded.

"Because sometimes a person has to wait until God takes the hurt away."

"So how'm I s'posed to help Jake? He's my friend." Sweet Alexa, trying to cheer up everyone.

"Sometimes the best thing we can do for people we love is to pray for them. Then we have to keep on loving them," Gemma explained.

"'Kay. Let's pray for Jake. Me first."

As this child launched into her heartfelt prayer for the man who'd befriended her, Gemma realized that the softness in her heart for Jake wasn't better or stronger or even taking the place of what she'd felt for Kurt. She *had* loved her husband. She knew that now after looking at the remnants of their life together. But it was a different love than what she felt for Jake; not better, not worse. Just different.

Kurt was Gemma's childhood love, a first love. These feelings she carried for Jake were that of an adult, colored by loss and the trials and struggles she'd weathered. She'd loved Kurt in a happy, discovering way. But her love for the man hurting in the deepest recesses of his heart because he couldn't resolve God's part in the deaths of his loved ones was cautious, not quite ready to be tested, new and a little frightening.

Despite his own pain, Jake kept willingly reaching out to help others. That was just one of many reasons why this man held her heart.

What would he do with it?

Chapter Twelve

That evening the children were already gathered around a campfire, waiting for their evening story time, when Jake arrived to hang the sheet that would be their screen.

Having finished that task, he slid onto a bench beside Alexa, reveling in her warm smile of welcome and the sweet rightness of her clambering onto his knee and looping one arm around his neck. Pain clutched his heart as old memories cascaded.

Oh, Thomas.

"I love you, Jake," Alexa whispered.

"I love you, too, sweetheart." He swallowed past the lump in his throat. "Do you like our movie screen? It works pretty well, doesn't it?" The glow of a glistening golden desert in the first light of morning blazed, waiting.

Gemma stood to one side, peering at her laptop. In her white jeans, green cotton shirt and sneakers, with her auburn hair plaited in two braids and wound around her head, she looked ready for a safari and so lovely it made his heart race.

Suddenly the low beat of drums filled the air. Jake, like the kids, stared at the screen, intrigued by flashing scenes of acacia trees, sand dunes, watering holes and herds of wild animals, obviously filmed from above by a drone or a plane.

"Welcome to Africa." Gemma inflected just the right blend of intrigue and tour guide into her speech. "This is a place where nothing is as it appears."

Everyone jumped when a huge lion roared directly into the camera. Giggles echoed around the valley.

She has them eating out of her hand, Jake thought. Then he, too, became caught up in her dialogue and visual displays.

"Some people say that Africa was the home of the garden of Eden, where God created Adam and Eve." History and geography wove together seamlessly in her presentation. "The people who live there now, the children of Africa, are like you. They want the same things you want. To love and care for their families, to have enough to eat, to run and play and laugh. To be safe."

As her pictures appeared and disappeared, Gemma's dialogue drew them deeper into the African world. She told them how these children's worlds were often torn apart and about how they had to learn to get along to live together. Jake marveled at the way she meshed pictures and stories, speaking of a young boy whose parents had died from disease, a young girl who'd lost an arm, children who didn't have enough food to eat. They were, she repeated, children just like those visiting The Haven, struggling to belong after having their lives turned upside down.

"When you think about fighting because someone calls you names, about disobeying your foster parents, about running away, think about Africa's children," Gemma murmured, holding each child's attention with her expressive voice. "Think about how God has blessed you with people who provide a home and food for you, who are doing the best they can to help you. Think about how much God loves you. And then think about how you could bless someone else, even if it's just to say something nice or do something simple like share your lunch."

"That's not much," a young boy said.

"It's a great deal," Gemma insisted. "That's how peace starts. You befriend someone and they befriend someone and soon there's no place for hurt or pain or anger among friends. You, my dear children, are God's hope for the future."

Now a video showed children sitting on the bare dirt, singing lustily, their smiles stretched wide. When they were finished and only the soft melody could still be heard, Gemma spoke again.

"When you think of Africa, remember that many of the kids you saw don't have things or money. That doesn't matter because things and money can't make you happy. Happiness comes from inside, from having God in your life, loving you, caring for you. It comes from caring for each other." She smiled, letting the words sink in before adding, "Let's each take one of these little drums and sing a song together, just like those kids did."

Alexa slid out of Jake's arms to retrieve her drum, and this time she stayed with the others as Gemma led the song in her clear soprano voice. Jake thought he'd never heard anything so lovely as the children's voices meshed with hers, lifted in worship. It was crystal clear to him that if she decided not to return to leading tours, Gemma had a definite ministry here at The Haven. The kids loved her.

So did he.

Jake sat frozen as the truth seeped from his heart into his head. He loved Gemma Andrews. Maybe he always had? Her strength, her convictions, her gentle soul and people-first attitude—they made Gemma who she was. The woman he loved.

Was it wrong to feel such love when he'd made that vow to Lily? Jake knew it was. Yet he couldn't quench his feelings. Neither could he act on them. He'd promised. So what *was* he supposed to do?

Jake wrestled with that question until all the kids had left, Alexa among them, to enjoy their evening snack. When they were alone, he stepped from the shadows and began to help Gemma clean up.

"That was wonderful." He folded the sheet thoughtfully. "You helped them see the world in a way that relates specifically to them."

"There are so many troubled kids here. I want to encourage them, to show them they aren't as poorly off as they think," she said quietly. "And that they aren't alone. It's a lesson the aunts struggled to teach me. How many times did they tell me to remember the names of God? My favorite is *Jehovah Jireh*, the God who provides."

That was the first of God's names that Jake had begun studying only a few days ago. His personal Bible study in the aunts' library was a feeble attempt at understanding God's nature, though Jake wasn't sure that was even possible. All he knew was that he couldn't go on as he had been, avoiding God and pretending to be something he wasn't.

Gemma's return to The Haven had made him see the futility of living a lie. Though he'd now studied three of God's names, understanding why God had acted as He had with Lily and Thomas was still a long way off.

"Let me carry that." Jake slipped the sheet

under one arm, grasped her laptop in his left hand and reached out with his right. "It's a steep climb here and the dew makes the grass slippery. Hang on to me."

"Thanks." Her hand slid into his, comfortable, warm. Perfect. She glanced up as they walked. "This sky is every bit as beautiful as an African one."

"You miss touring," he said, understanding the soft, yearning expression.

"Sometimes. Especially when I see my pictures again." She smiled and shook her head. "But then I talk to the aunts or my sisters or spend time with the kids and I think, what could be better than this? The Haven is a true refuge. Foster kids come here defensive, hurting, needy, and slowly they're able to find hope again as they learn about God. This ministry of Aunt Tillie and Aunt Margaret's is amazing."

"It is," he agreed.

"Speaking of missing things. Do you ever yearn to be back in a greenhouse, Jake, working entirely with plants?" Gemma stopped in a shaft of moonlight, inquisitive green eyes wide in her oval face.

"I've never considered it." He did now. He *could* return to horticulture, start his own business again, but would it ever fulfill him as much as his work at The Haven and his projects in Chokecherry Hollow? Would he ever find a partner like Gemma?

"Not that I'm suggesting you should leave here," she said soberly, her gaze intense. "I'd miss you, Jake. You're very special to me."

Those words and the concentration of her stare reminded him of her avowal of love. He hesitated, wanting to remind her that nothing could come of that, but she chuckled before he could respond.

"Besides, you'd be terribly hard to replace."

Jake didn't laugh. In fact, he barely heard her next words because a new thought struck him. If Gemma stayed, perhaps he *should* leave. It would be much easier to keep his vow if he didn't constantly see her.

Not see Gemma every day, not hear her full-bodied laughter, not watch her teach Alexa and the other kids how to embrace the world and trust God? No!

His heart sank. What would give meaning to his days if Gemma wasn't there?

"Jake? Are you asleep?" She peered at him, her face inches away.

It took every ounce of control Jake possessed not to breach the distance between them and kiss her.

"Jake?" Her fingers tightened around his arm.

"No," he said slowly. "I'm not asleep."

"Good. No one should sleep through a star shower like this." She slid her hand free and lifted her eyes to the heavens. *"Elohim,"* she whispered. "God of power and might."

Another name of God. For a moment Jake wondered if she knew of his Bible study. But how? He'd been so careful to sneak into the library in the early morning, long before any-one else was stirring. Then he recalled that she'd once said she'd learned God's names from her aunts.

He stood beside her for a long time, savor-ing these precious moments alone together, knowing he couldn't allow it to happen again.

"I do care about you, Jake." Gemma's voice pierced the silence around them as her gaze rested on him. "Maybe you think it's wrong for me to say that so soon after Kurt's death." Her green eyes were clear and focused. "It doesn't feel wrong. I know that I loved Kurt. Maybe not enough, maybe not as I should have, but I did love him."

"Like you love me?" He hated that he'd asked that question, like some needy youth who craved reassurance. Yet nothing could have stopped it because he needed to know.

Gemma shook her head slowly from left to right.

"No, I don't love you like I did Kurt."

"Because no one can replace him in your life," he rushed to say, desperate to force her to face the truth before it led to something he couldn't derail. "You're vulnerable and you have a crush on me. You even said that."

But Gemma shook her head again, and this time tears welled in her eyes. Jake clenched his fists to stop himself from embracing her.

"I said I *had* a crush once. This is different. You can ignore it. You can pretend it's a crush if you want to," she whispered. "But that won't change how I feel now. I know my heart and it says I'm in love with you."

"But Gem." Jake raked a hand through his hair, wishing he'd avoided this entire scene. He didn't want to hurt her but neither did he want her to continue with this fantasy world. "I can't," he began.

She placed her fingers over his lips.

"I know. You made a vow." She removed her hand and tilted her head sideways. "Why did you make that vow, Jake?"

"Why?" He frowned in confusion. "I told you—"

"Yes, yes. You felt guilty after Lily's and Thomas's deaths." She nodded. "Got that. So the vow was like your atonement? A kind of self-punishment?"

"What?" He stared at her, aghast. "No! It wasn't about me."

"Well then why?" she pressed. "I mean, why vow that? Why not take flowers to Lily's grave every month or work on making your business the best it could be in honor of them?"

"My *business* is what got them killed," Jake snarled, more irritated than he'd been in years.

"No. Carbon monoxide killed your wife and child. Maybe because of a faulty detector or maybe because of a defect in the fireplace, or perhaps both." Her voice was firm. "*You* did not kill them. Nor can you take responsibility for the storm that waylaid you."

Jake couldn't say anything, couldn't argue

with her because he couldn't, *would not* follow where she was leading. So he remained
silent, waiting for her to finish whatever she
had to say so he could leave, hide out in his
cabin and pretend Gem's love was all one-
sided.

"I understand you were hurting terribly. To
lose your beloved family that way—" Tears
glossed her eyes as she silently wept. "I'm
so sorry, Jake. So very sorry. Please believe
that I'm not in any way trying to diminish
your loss."

He inclined his head in acceptance but he
said nothing, because he dared not.

"What I don't understand is your response
to their deaths. Why would you believe that
never letting anyone into your life again,
never allowing anyone to get close to you,
to share your journey, would take away the
pain?" Gemma stared at her clasped hands.
"I know that blaming yourself is natural.
Perhaps it even helped for a while. But to
make that vow..." Suddenly her head lifted

and she looked directly at him, green eyes wide. "Is your vow something God told you to do?"

"I didn't talk to God for years after their deaths," he snapped. "Except to ask why. There was never an answer so I soon stopped asking even that."

Not true. In his heart he still asked why. Maybe always would.

"So this atonement of yours," she murmured. "How does it help you or them?"

"It helps ensure that I will never risk any woman's life again, let alone a child's." Jake glared at her. "It helps me live with the guilt and the pain."

Gemma looked at him with pity though she said nothing.

"Are we done here?" he demanded. "Because I need to take this to the house and then finish up a job or two."

"I don't think your vow is helping you, Jake. I think you suppress your real feelings by rushing around here, helping everybody, looking after the townsfolk, spending time with me. I think your vow is your excuse to stay emotionally untouched and avoid all the pain that entails." She pressed her lips together but Jake knew she wasn't finished with him.

"You might as well say it all, Gem." Maybe then they could move on.

"I will. One of the names of God that I've been relying on since the earthquake is Jehovah *Rapha*, the Lord that heals. It's an amazing name." She reached out and brushed her hand against his cheek in the most tender caress. "Why don't you try talking to God the healer, Jake? Why don't you find out what He wants and expects from you? Why don't you let Him heal the load of guilt you're carrying so you can finally be free?"

Then, without another word, Gemma hurried into the darkness.

Jake stood there, her words echoing inside his head, wondering what it would be like to live without the constant cloak of culpability that had dogged him for seven long years.

"What's wrong, Gem?"

A week later Alexa's question and the soft squeeze of her hug drew Gemma from her misery.

"Are you sad 'cause Jake don't wanna be with us no more? 'Cause he don't love us no more?" The pathos in Alexa's voice smacked Gemma in the heart.

"Sweetheart, Jake loves you very much." She brushed the newly trimmed curls off the little girl's forehead.

"Then why din't he come with us on our picnic?" Alexa demanded.

"He said he's too busy today," Gemma excused though she knew it wasn't the truth.

"Jake's not busy. I heard him talking to that Mr. Billy, tellin' him he was coming for coffee 'cause he was bored." Big tears rolled down her cheeks. "I prayed an' prayed like the aunties tole me, but Jake don't like me no more. That's why he's going away."

"Jake is leaving?" Gemma's heart sank. "When?"

"I dunno." Alexa sniffed. "But I heard the aunties say he's running. I thought he liked it at The Haven. I thought he liked me. But why does he wanna go 'way if he does?"

Truth time.

"It's not you he wants to get away from, honey. It's me," she admitted. "Jake and I had a disagreement."

"You fighted?" Alexa frowned. "How come?"

"It wasn't exactly a fight." Gemma sighed, searching for the right words. "I said something he didn't like so now he's staying away from me."

"Did you talk 'bout his little boy?" Alexa asked and sighed when Gemma nodded. "He don't like it when I talk 'bout Thomas neither. This morning I seed him lookin' at a picture of a baby, maybe like Thomas. Jake was sad, so I gave him a hug. I tol' him God and me loved him and that you did, too."

"I'm sure he liked the hug, sweetie, but why did you say that about me?"

"'Cause it's true. You do love Jake. I knowed it," she said simply. "Mommy tole me you can always tell when somebody loves somebody by how they act. Jake 'n you act like you love each other."

"I do love Jake, Alexa, but he doesn't love me." Man, it hurt to say that.

"Does so." Alexa planted her hands on her hips.

"No, sweetie." Gemma knew Alexa wasn't convinced. "He told me he can't love me. I guess he's still too sad about his family dying."

"Uh-uh." The little girl stubbornly shook her head. Then she flopped down in the tall grass. She grabbed a stem to chew on. "Jake loves you lots, Gem."

I wish. But after much prayer and consultations with her aunts, Gemma had finally accepted that she didn't belong here, didn't belong with Jake. No matter how much she wished she did.

"I knowed he loves you when I seed him put our flowers in that jar on your table." Alexa nodded at her surprised look. "An' I knowed it when he moved those benches around the fire so everybody could see your pictures more better. An' when he went huntin' for that ribbon you lost outta your hair yesterday, I knowed it, too. Jake loves you lots."

"As a friend," Gemma said, nonplused by the child's observations. "That's all. Can I explain something to you, sweetie?"

She waited for Alexa's nod while searching for a way to tell this very precious child that she'd decided to leave The Haven and resume her career of traveling the world. But she couldn't bring herself to do it. Alexa might think Gemma had stopped loving her, too, and she didn't want to hurt the child.

Instead she taught the little girl a game that

tired them both so much, they happily plodded back to The Haven to enjoy an afternoon snack. Alexa stuck close by her side, clinging to her hand and refusing to join the other kids, as she'd recently begun to do.

Later that night, after Gemma had finished her presentation, she tucked Alexa into bed, listened to her prayers and kissed the little girl good-night. She was sitting in the shadowed corner of the patio, staring at the stars, when she noticed Jake sneak into the house. She knew he was going to see Alexa. He did every night.

How could she leave here, leave Jake and Alexa, the two people who, along with her aunts and her sisters, were now an integral part of her world? How would Alexa manage without someone to love her, to constantly assure her that she was not alone, that she belonged?

How would Gemma face days and nights alone, always on the outside, always wishing she belonged to someone? To Jake.

"Please make Your will clear to me," she prayed silently. "If I must leave, show me how to tell Alexa so she won't be hurt. And please, be with Jake. He needs You now more than he ever has."

Gemma sat praying until long after Jake had left, long after the moon had slid across the sky to give way to the first pink rays of dawn. When she finally rose and went to her room, her heart ached no less.

I could have belonged here, with Jake, she said to herself. *Will I ever belong anywhere?*

Chapter Thirteen

As it turned out, having Sweetie the cow wasn't as bad as Jake had thought. She listened to him rant without comment or argument the entire time he cleaned her barn. Her one failure was that she had no advice to offer.

"So you think I should go? I mean, The Haven has been home for a long time. I hate to leave the aunts, especially after all they've done for me."

Sweetie swung her head from side to side.

"You don't? You know there are tons of helpers with this ministry now and any one of them could do what I do, especially feed you. The thing is—Gem's here. If I stay I know I won't be able to keep that vow. She's dug herself into my heart."

Sweetie mooed.

"Yeah. You're right. I do need to leave. I'll tell the aunts today and plan to take off on the weekend. It will be better for Gem that way."

"Who are you talkin' to, Jake?" Alexa's high-pitched voice inquired as she peeked around the barn door. "An' what's better for Gem?"

He couldn't tell her the truth. She'd blab and things would get very uncomfortable. To divert her attention, Jake handed her an apple to feed the cow.

"Aren't you going riding today?" he asked.

"Yep. That's why I got my boots on." Alexa stuck out her foot to show him. Then she asked, "Are you still mad at Gem?"

"I was never mad at Gemma, Alexa." He smiled at the little girl who'd wiggled her way into his heart. "We just disagree on some things."

"Mommy said that if you love someone you look for ways to make you both happy," she said sagely. "You're makin' Gem sad."

"I wish I could fix that, honey, but I can't," Jake said.

"I know." She exhaled a heavy sigh. "'Cause you're sad, too. I gotta pray 'bout you both some more, I guess."

"You've been praying for Gemma and me?" he asked in surprise.

"O' course." She gave him her *Alexa* look, the one that was both stern and sweet. "Don't you?"

"I guess." Though he'd muttered some type of prayer for himself and Gemma individually many times, he'd never thought of praying for their joint concerns—as a couple.

Why don't you try talking to God again?

What he'd been doing could hardly be called praying.

"There's the whistle. I gotta go get on the bus." Alexa reached her arms up to him for a hug.

Jake bent, throat constricting as her chubby

hands stretched around his neck and pulled him close. He held her tenderly, as if she was a fragile butterfly.

"See you later, honey," he managed to say while his brain drew pictures of what Thomas might have been like at this age. He wondered whether his son would have hugged his dad so tightly.

"I love you, Jake." Alexa pressed a kiss against his cheek. "Kurt tol' me we gotta make sure to say that 'cause you never know when you won't see somebody again." She eyed him with a stern look. "You're not goin' away 'fore I finish riding, are you?"

She knew he was leaving? Shocked, Jake shook his head.

"Good. 'Cause I got things I needa tell you." Alexa fluttered a hand and then raced away.

Jake sank onto a bale and tried to sort out his whirling thoughts.

Why don't you try talking to God again?

"God? Are You there?" Silly question. God

was always there. "I haven't really talked to You in a long time. I've pretended to. I've yelled at You." He paused. "I've missed You. I miss them."

The tears fell and for once he let them, let the sorrow fill his heart.

"I can barely remember them," he whispered. "I have to keep looking at their pictures to remind myself. Is that love?"

"Yes, Jake, it is." Aunt Tillie sat on the bale next to him, her voice gentle and comforting. "When we love someone and they pass away, all we have left are memories. We still cherish them, of course, always will. But eventually we have to move on with our lives, into our future. Because clinging to the past stops us from experiencing all the wonder that God has planned for us."

"But I loved them," he protested.

"Of course you did, dear. And they loved you. But they're gone now. Not forgotten, just gone." She studied him with an intensity that made Jake uncomfortable. "Would Lily

want you to be stuck in the past, to never experience love again? To never know the love
of another child?"

"You don't understand," he muttered. "I
promised."

"You promised never to love anyone
again?" Tillie shook her head. "You said that
out of some feeling that it could atone for
them dying, Jake. Because you blame yourself for their deaths. That is very wrong of
you," she said sternly.

"Wrong?" He jerked upright and stared at
her. "Why?"

"Because when we're God's children, He
is in charge of everything. He's God." Tillie's voice softened. "The name *Adonai* is a
name for God that means Lord, Master. You
don't question your lord and master."

"I guess not." Jake tried to assimilate that.

"From the little you've told Margaret and
me, Lily loved God. He decided she and
Thomas would be better off with Him. As
our Lord, He has the right to decide what

happens in our lives, even if it means taking our loved ones. But that doesn't mean He abandoned you." She folded her hands in her lap, her face placid. "I think God brought love into your life when you came to The Haven."

These aunties… They always seemed to see beneath to the root of the problem. Jake wasn't sure how to respond.

"You've loved Gemma for a long time, haven't you?" she murmured.

What was the point in denying it?

"Yes."

"Yes. And because she loved Kurt back then she was no threat to your self-imposed isolation. Now she is because she loves you, and that demands a response. Your response is to run." Tillie patted his hand as if to reassure him. "I do believe Gemmie truly loves you, Jake. It's not a reaction to all she's gone through. It's not a whim or a flight of fancy. She cares deeply about you."

"Gemma told you this?"

"She didn't have to, dear. It's written all over her face when she sees you, talks about you." The older woman's smile warmed his spirit. "Her eyes light up as brightly as a thousand stars. Her whole demeanor changes when she sees you. She plans things with you in mind. She shares your outreach to the needy in Chokecherry Hollow because she enjoys it, of course. But also because she loves being with you, working with you. Gemma loves *you*."

"She can't," Jake blurted.

"Not that you saying that alters her love one whit," Tillie reminded with a chuckle. "But why can't she?"

"Because I'm leaving The Haven." He let it hang there for a moment, surprised by how sad those words made him feel.

"I guessed that would be your reaction." Tillie sighed. "The Haven's been your home for six years. We've been very blessed to have you. You've done so much to make our lives easier, as well as many in our surrounding area. We've all come to count on you, Jake. You've been a rich and special blessing." Tillie's words were gentle, yet oddly unemotional.

"Thank you," he murmured, moved by her comments.

"If you now feel God is leading you away from here, we will miss you greatly, but we will send you forward into new experiences with our blessings and a promise to pray for you."

"I appreciate that." A hollow sensation filled his gut that Aunt Tillie didn't argue, didn't try to persuade him not to go. "I'll leave on Saturday. Can you please keep it quiet until after I've left? I don't want anyone to know."

"Because you don't want to face Gemma's tears. Or Alexa's. You think that if you pass quietly into the night, that will make it easier for them." Tillie shook her head. "It won't. It might make it easier for you, but it will only leave them with a lot of unanswered questions. Still, if that is your decision, Margaret and I will abide by it."

"Thank you." The older woman rose. So did Jake.

"We love you, Jake. We have from that first day we saw you sitting on the corner of that street in Edmonton. You were contemplating suicide, weren't you?"

He blinked. "How did you know?"

"It's a God thing." She shrugged. "May I say one more thing?"

"Of course." *Please don't talk about Gemma. It hurts too much.*

"Promise me that you'll seek God, find out if this truly is the plan He has in mind for you or if you're simply running away again, just like you did after your family's deaths."

"Hey!" Jake burst out angrily. "I didn't run away."

"Didn't you, dear?" Tillie's sage look bugged him. "I think you started running the day you chose to make that vow and I don't believe you've stopped since. But sooner or later God will have to stop your self-destruction. Because He loves you. I pray that happens before you throw away everything precious He's given you. You belong at The Haven, Jake. I hope you come to see that. We love you."

After a tender embrace, Tillie left. Sometime later the lunch bell rang, but Jake ignored it, just like he ignored the self-doubts that now filled him. Tillie was mistaken. He hadn't been wrong to make that vow to Lily. He owed it to her memory not to risk Gemma's life by loving her.

Desperate to be rid of the merry-go-round of questions, Jake focused on finishing the chores he'd left till 'sometime.' He wanted everything in order before he left. It was the least he could do for the sweet aunties.

He was almost finished repairing a section of the garden fence when the weather warning chimed on his phone. With chagrin he read about a severe storm approaching the area including The Haven. Dangerously high winds and fierce rain were predicted. Perhaps hail. He called Victoria.

"Yes, I got it. We need to gather all the kids inside The Haven. Now," she said.

"Okay, I'll do a run, chase whomever I find to the house. The riding group?" he asked, thinking of Alexa.

"They just returned." That response relieved his worry until she continued. "There's a hiking group in the valley that I can't reach. They're probably exploring the old cave. Can you take the quad and ensure they get back safely? I'll start checking off names so we know who else is still missing."

"Gemma could help me with that." Always she was there in his head, his mind, his heart.

"She's not here. I think she's looking through some stuff Alexa's social worker sent today. I'll find her. Be safe."

"You, too, Vic. See you in a bit."

Jake drove the four-wheeler toward the hiking trails. Fortunately the hiking group's leader had received the warning and was leading them home though they struggled to hurry against the now very brisk wind.

Jake loaded the three slowest kids on his quad and tailed the group until they arrived safely at The Haven. He helped gather other stragglers to safety, made sure Sweetie was sheltered securely in the barn and chased the aunts' rescue dogs, Spot and Dot, into the house.

Jake was almost finished securing the patio furniture when Alexa yelled at him through the open kitchen window. He hurried inside and locked the window.

"Honey, you can't open the windows. The wind's—"

"Gem's not here, Jake," the little girl sobbed. "We gotta go find her."

"You can't go out in this wind, Alexa. It's too dangerous. There's stuff flying all over." He tamped down his fears and bent to her level. "Tell me when you last saw her."

"When we comed back on the bus from

riding, I seed her walking. She was far away. She din't hear me call her." Alexa's tears washed her white face. "I thought she'd come back but she din't. Victoria says it's a really bad storm. We gotta go find Gemma."

His heart in his throat, Jake texted Victoria. She replied she hadn't seen her sister. Jake's worry ramped up. But one peek out the window showed debris whirling crazily, ripping flowers and bushes out of the ground. He wasn't taking a child out in that.

"Jake, can you come help us close the shutters in the library? I'm so glad we had them installed inside so we could watch movies. It will keep us safe and help entertain the children." Aunt Margaret went to Alexa and took her hand. "Come on, sweetie. We'll all ask God to keep our Gemmie safe before the movie starts."

Jake helped Olivia secure the library windows so that even if the glass was broken, it would not fall inside and injure a child. When the power failed, he turned on the backup generator that he'd filled earlier. He waited while the entire group prayed for Gemma's safety. The movie started, but it seemed to take a long time for kids to settle. Jake slipped out to the kitchen to ask Adele to make some popcorn, hoping a snack might help take their minds off the storm. It did.

But as the winds whined higher outside, his worries wouldn't quiet. Where was Gemma? Had she received the warning, taken shelter? Was she safe? He needed to find her, but with the ladies and kids huddled inside The Haven, and without the sisters' husbands here to help, Jake couldn't leave. His job was to protect these vulnerable ones, even if it was the last thing he did before he left.

"We've prayed for Gemma, Jake," Margaret murmured as they sat in the kitchen, enjoying the coffee Adele had brewed on the big gas stove. "And we'll continue praying. But we need to talk." Her stern voice brooked no argument.

"About?" *Where is Gemma?*

"About your vow to Lily. Sister told me of your conversation in the barn." Margaret shook her head at him. "I first need to know one thing. Do you truly love Gemma?"

"Yes." Jake couldn't have stopped that response if he'd wanted to. "And I need to find her. Now," he said shoving away his cup. He was halfway risen when Tillie's hand pressed downward.

"God is looking after Gemma. He's looking after all of us." Tillie's tender smile expressed her supreme confidence in her Father. "Even you."

"That vow of yours, Jake. I need to say this." Margaret's frown was fierce. "It was so wrong."

"Huh?" Jake demanded. "Tillie said that, too. Why is it wrong?"

"Because it shows your lack of trust in our heavenly Father and that must wound Him terribly." Margaret leaned forward. "God loves us. We're His children. He doesn't ask us to sacrifice something so we can get back in His good graces after bad things happen. God never asked you to give up loving someone after Lily died."

"No, I made that decision," he agreed. "Because my neglect—"

"Stop that." For the first time since he'd met her, Margaret's eyes flashed with anger. "Were Lily and Thomas not God's children?" Jake nodded. "Then He was their Lord and He was in control of their lives. Not you."

"My dear boy, your vow came from a place of guilt. It wasn't something from God. Why do you think He led us to you, led you to The Haven to help us when we so badly needed help? Why do you think He laid it on your heart to get involved in our community?" Tillie held up a hand, forestalling his objections. "And don't say it's because you're no good at anything else. God gave you specific talents for a specific purpose, my boy. Nothing is random with God. He has a plan. Always."

"Giving up love doesn't help anyone, especially not you." Margaret's softened tone made her comments easier to accept. "Cherishing love and lavishing it on others helps everyone, giver and receiver. Isn't that why you've been helping folks in Chokecherry Hollow, because you feel better for doing it?"

Jake nodded as their words percolated through his brain.

"You love Gemma, don't you?" Margaret asked.

"Yes. But I'm not sure it matters anymore," he mumbled. "She's talking of leaving."

"With God it is never too late." Tillie rested her hand on his shoulder. "You understand now that your vow was your way of keeping your heart safe, don't you?"

"I'm not sure—"

"The Bible says that if we lack wisdom we should ask God and He will give it. Let's do that now."

Jake bowed his head, listening to the sisters pray for him, for Gemma, for everyone at The Haven. As he did, understanding filled his soul until at last the heavy cloak of guilt that had weighed him down for seven long years, quietly melted away.

He didn't have to worry about Lily and Thomas. They were with God. Finally he could let go of the past.

Gemma had spent the most glorious afternoon simply wandering the familiar hills and letting their peace and serenity soothe her aching soul. She finally arrived at her favorite spot, a wooded grove where she'd so often found solace as a teen. Weary in mind and body, and desperate for answers, she sat below the giant spruce and poured out her heart to God.

"Jake cares for me. I know he does." But then she recalled her uncle and how he'd embezzled the funds his own brother had left for his child. If her own blood relative couldn't love her enough to stop his greed, how could anyone else?

In that instant her old nemesis of insecurity took control. *You love The Haven but you don't belong here, not anymore—if you ever did.*

So, telling stories—was that all she was good for?

"What do You want me to do?" she prayed aloud. "I could go back to touring. I'm good at it. I'll have opportunities to talk to people about Your world. They want me back."

But was it where she *belonged*?

"If I stay here, I can be with kids, invite Alexa more often, build a closer relationship with her." *Maybe even adopt her?*

Would that make her belong?

"If I stayed I could make Your world come alive for the kids who come. Maybe help them figure out their futures." *When you can't even figure out your own?*

A crack of lightning roused Gemma from her thoughts. Suddenly aware that the sky was now black and sending a sprinkle of rain, and that the wind was blowing with fierce abandon, she hurried to find shelter in the cleft of a rocky promontory. There, protected from the elements, she leaned her back against the granite and watched the storm play out in front of her, amazed at the awesome power and strength of the elements.

The turbulence was breathtaking. It made her feel small and insignificant, a mere speck in the chaos around her. Which she was. And yet God was in control. He wasn't upset or confused or worried by the storm. He knew just how much the trees in front of her could bend and sway in the gale-force winds without breaking.

In an instant He could stop those spears of lightning and end the sheets of white hail spewing from the heavens. He knew exactly how long it would take for the barrage of frozen stones to melt and turn to rivers that gushed downward.

Gemma felt like she stood in the middle of a crazy whirlwind that was wreaking havoc, and yet it was all under God's control. Just as the earthquake had been.

Then it was over.

Gemma remained transfixed as the first colors of a rainbow snuck across the sky and spread into multicolored glistening ribbons. The arch somehow echoed the memory of a song. Her mother's song, she suddenly realized. She could almost hear that long-silenced voice crooning the words of her favorite hymn.

This is my Father's world.

Yes, He was in control of everything. Yes, He'd saved her from an earthquake and yes, He'd brought her home. Because The Haven *was* home. This *was* where Gemma belonged. Her travels had shown her the glories of her Father's world so she could share it with kids who needed to hear of His love. She wasn't giving up anything. She was stepping into a whole new challenge, one God had given her. Because He believed in her.

Yes, she loved Jake with her whole heart.

She desperately wanted him to love her. But that was in God's hands, too. Just as He managed the wind and the rain, and the rainbow, so He could be trusted to manage her future. If she was not to be with Jake, then she would, with His help, learn to deal with that.

Because not only was she home at The Haven, she was at home in God.

Gemma stepped out into the sun and lifted her face to the heavens.

"I will trust in You," she said, loud and strong and firm.

Then she began walking toward The Haven. And Jake.

Chapter Fourteen

Jake struggled without success to get Alexa to stop crying. Finally, so she wouldn't disturb the other children, he took her up to her room.

"What are all these boxes?" he asked, easing one out of the way so he could set the little girl on her bed.

"Mommy's an' my stuff. Gem was gonna help me make a book." And off she went again, crying for Gemma.

The ladies were all busy managing things downstairs. It was up to him to handle this. Jake knelt in front of Alexa and cupped her chin in his.

"Want to hear my idea?"

She sniffed and nodded.

"I think you and I should begin this book as a surprise for Gemma when she comes back." He glanced around as if he was confused and didn't know how to begin. "Do you want all this stuff in your book?"

"No, silly. Jus' pictures." She brushed away the tears with the back of her hand and then hunkered down on the carpet, peeking into each box until she came to the last one. "Mommy made this book. It's a baby book. See. That's me." Alexa seemed to forget Gemma as she pointed out herself at varying ages.

But Jake couldn't forget. He kept glancing out the window, not wanting to think of Gem caught in the midst of that terrifying wind. He prayed desperately that she'd found a safe place to hide.

"My mommy's really pretty, isn't she?" Alexa's fingers traced a woman's face.

"She's beautiful, sweetheart. I think hers

should be the first picture." Fortunately someone, probably Gemma, had left a new photograph album on the small desk by the window. Jake handed Alexa a glue stick. "You put it where you think it looks best."

Now totally involved, Alexa took the glue stick, opened the album and began gluing picture after picture, carefully placing each on a page. She asked him to print the names underneath.

"In case I forget," she said sadly.

"I don't think you'll forget, sweetheart," he reassured. "But even if you do, you can always look here and remember."

"Yeah." She chuckled at the next snapshot. "Kurt din't fly my kite good. It crashed. He was gonna gived me a new one." Her face fell. "Now he can't."

"I can. You and I will pick one out tomorrow. Okay?" Why had he tried to shelve his memories? Suddenly he wanted to retrieve the photo albums Lily had so carefully assembled. He needed to see her lovely face and Thomas's grumpy frown and remember the joy they'd brought to his world.

"Are you still sad, Jake?" Alexa leaned her head on his arm.

"Not really," he said and realized it was true. He felt blessed that he'd been able to share their lives, even if only for such a short time. "I was just thinking about Thomas and trying to remember what he looked like."

"Don'cha got no pictures?" she demanded.

"Yes, sweetheart, I do." Jake lifted her onto his lap and hugged her.

"Where?" Alexa wasn't about to give up. "I wanna see. You seed mine."

"I have them put away in a box," he explained.

"Well, that's silly." She shook her head. "How you gonna remember 'em if you keep 'em in a box?" She released a heavy sigh. "Sometimes I think grownups are kinda dumb."

"Me, too," he agreed.

As soon as the storm was over, Jake was

going to open that box and take out that family picture. Every time he looked at it, he'd remind himself of how blessed he'd been to have such a wonderful chapter in the book of his life.

That's when Jake realized that his story wasn't over. There were more pages to come in his life-album, another chapter he needed to include because he'd been blessed again by love. It didn't compete with Lily, just as Gemma's love for Kurt didn't compete with hers for him. Each was beautiful in and of itself. Jake could accept that now. It was like his rosebushes. One branch might die, but life returned on another branch, and if treated properly, it flourished and produced wonderful roses.

He could hardly wait to tell Gemma of his newly garnered understanding.

Alexa had been repeatedly dabbing the glue stick and plopping photos onto each page. But suddenly she stopped.

"This is my 'nother fav'rite," she whispered. "See how Gem's smiling?"

"I sure do." Jake remembered the occasion as if it was yesterday. The three of them were trying to get Sweetie to go into the barn. Successive failed attempts had sent Gemma into peals of laughter. "I think it's my 'nother fav'rite, too," Jake whispered.

"'Cause you love Gem." Alexa nodded. "I knowed it a long time ago," she said wisely and patted his cheek. Then her eyes widened. "Hey, lookit, Jake. The sun's shinin'. The storm's all done."

Someone called up the stairs for them to come outside.

Jake walked with Alexa out to the lawn where they had the best vantage point of the valley and the Rockies beyond. Among children and adults, with Alexa's hand clasped in his, Jake gazed at the beautiful rainbow stretching across the sky.

Thank you, Father. Peace calmed his soul. Yet still his heart asked, *Where is Gemma?*

As Jake scanned his surroundings and absorbed the amount of damage the storm had wreaked, fear began to move in. Broken branches littered the ground, along with shingles ripped off damaged outbuilding roofs. Had she been hit by one of them? Flower pots had been sent tumbling in the wind and now lay smashed in scattered shards, with dirt oozing out. Several outbuildings would require extensive repair, including the shed that had housed Gem's belongings such a short time ago.

It didn't matter because Jake would be here to do it all, with God's help.

"I have to go hunt for Gemma now," he told Alexa.

"Nope, you don't gotta." She giggled.

"Why not?" He frowned as he followed her pointing finger. For a moment his heart sank to his toes. His garden was a mess of balled-up fencing and uprooted plants. The entire area had been decimated by the wind and the hail. The greenhouse lay a flattened ruin of shattered glass, his roses crushed.

"She's there," Alexa squealed.

That's when Jake spotted Gemma crouched beside the broken stalks of corn, her long hair tumbling over her shoulders, dirt sifting through her fingers as she examined the carnage.

Thank you, God.

"Wait here, Alexa," he said sternly. "I need to make sure the glass didn't blow around."

"'Kay. But hurry 'cause I think she's cryin'."

Jake raced toward Gemma, fighting the fear threatening to fill his soul until he remembered the aunts' words. God was in charge.

"Gem?"

"It's ruined," she sobbed, lifting her head to stare at him. Her gorgeous green eyes brimmed with tears. "All your hard work and Alexa's pretty flowers. The raspberry canes you started, the peas the kids were going to pick tomorrow and the roses—the poor roses. There's nothing left of them. I'm so sorry, Jake."

"They'll grow again, Gem. This was just a pruning." Slowly, tenderly, Jake slid his fingers under her elbow and drew her upright to hold her in front of him. "Look at the rainbow," he whispered in her ear. "Look at the promise God's given us. Not that bad things won't happen. But that He will be there with us through all of it."

She turned to face him, eyes dark with confusion. "Don't you care about the garden?"

"We can plant again, Gem. We'll clean this up, rake the soil and start over. Isn't that what life is about? Renewal." The confident words came easily to him now.

"I—I don't understand."

Her confused whisper touched his heart. Jack wrapped his arms around her and smiled, finally free to open his heart.

"I do. I was like that garden. I felt like I'd been ripped up and torn open. I was sure nothing could ever grow in my heart again." Seeing the barrenness of his life with new perspective shocked Jake. "But God the gardener has been working on me, showing me that I was wallowing in my own loss instead of depending on Him to help me get through it."

"I—I…" She gave up and simply studied him, waiting.

"I love you, Gemma. I have for a very long time, though I couldn't accept it, couldn't see it as anything but a betrayal of Lily because I'd let guilt take over my mind." He shook his head. "I was going to run away from here, try to bury my unhappiness." He smiled. "I may eventually leave, but only if you're going, too. God will have to move us together because I intend to be wherever you are, sharing His love, reaching out to other people."

"Say all of it," she murmured when he paused.

"I want to marry you, Gem. I want us to adopt Alexa because she belongs with us. I want us to make a home here or nearby, close enough that we can continue to be part of The Haven's amazing ministry, part of the community." Jake let the dream expand in his mind. "Kids need love. Everyone needs God's love. We all need to understand the power of that love to work in us and through us so we can help others."

Gemma's continued silence was nerve-racking.

"Aren't you going to say anything?" he finally demanded, exasperated.

"Darling Jake." Her hand lifted so her fingers could trace the lines of his face. "I love you so much. I love the way you put people first, the way you cherish Alexa, my family and every single kid who comes to this place. I would be honored to marry you and continue working with you. We've proven, have we not, that we are a pretty amazing partnership?"

"You're sure?" But Jake saw the truth on her face.

"Doubting me already?"

"Never." He bent his head and kissed her, trying to infuse all his hopes and dreams for their future together into that embrace. He must have succeeded, because Gemma kissed him back, fully, completely, her response more wonderful than anything he could have ever dared dream. When they finally drew apart, Jake tilted back to get a better look at her face.

"Tell me," he said simply.

"I was watching the storm from this cave, marveling at God's awesome power. Then it was over and suddenly I just knew that staying at The Haven is God's plan for me, whether or not you were here." Her arms tightened around his neck. "I love you dearly, but I had to trust you to God, my darling Jake, if I wanted to be able to give back just a small portion of what He's blessed me with."

She kissed him once more and Jake couldn't have cared less that kids and adults alike were applauding.

"I'm sorry it took me so long to figure

out who's in charge in this world," he murmured, loving the silken length of her hair in his fingers.

"Time God used very well," Gem reminded. "So don't regret it. Let's embrace our future with full hearts." She touched his cheek. "We must adopt Alexa. Kurt would be so happy to see his precious little girl in our family. Together we'll make sure she always knows she's loved. As I will you, my darling Jake."

"And I you." He kissed her again. Then he took her hand and led her through the tangled mess and out the gate to where Alexa waited.

"You sure kiss a lot," the little girl charged grumpily as she clung to Gemma's legs. "Everything got ruined and you're happy 'bout it."

"No, sweetie." Jake hunkered down to her level and brushed his lips against her cheek. "We're happy because we love each other and we're getting married and we want to adopt you as our daughter." He grinned at her. "Is that okay with you?"

"So I c'n stay here forever?" Alexa's big blue eyes glanced from him to Gemma, who nodded. Alexa squealed with joy, until she noticed the garden. "But what 'bout my flowers?"

"They'll come back, sweetheart. They're perennials," he explained. "That means they keep seeding each year so new flowers can grow."

"It's just like God's promises," Gemma added. "That's what the rainbow means, that God will always love us, always be here to help us."

"I'm stayin' here." Alexa hugged herself. Then, after a last mournful look at her dying flowers, she slid her tiny hands into theirs. "C'n we 'dopt other kids? I like Charlotte an' Benjamin best, but maybe Jordan would be a good brother. An' David's nice." She kept listing children she thought would make great siblings.

Jake grinned at Gemma.

"So this is what it's going to be like," he murmured.

"Uh-huh." Her megawatt smile lit up her face. "Isn't it wonderful?"

"Yep." He threw her a sly grin. "If we're going to adopt all these kids we'd better get married soon. Tomorrow?"

They negotiated the deal later that evening, on the patio. Without onlookers.

Chapter Fifteen

Gemma Andrews married Jake Elliot on the third Saturday in August. It was supposed to be an intimate wedding with only family and friends.

Turned out, the couple had a lot of friends.

From far and wide, folks who'd been touched by or helped by the couple's community outreach kept visiting The Haven. Each came laden with lush potted plants, cut flowers and beautiful hanging baskets that transformed the ravaged area into a gorgeous wedding venue. Even the garden looked spectacular because Gemma's sisters had transformed it by having their husbands lay artificial turf and add an airy white gazebo.

On the morning of the wedding all was ready. Among stalks of vibrant gladioli which Billy had cut fresh from Ethel's garden, rows of white chairs waited for guests, joined by satin ropes and bows in Gemma's favorite shade of blue—to match her fiancé's eyes. In front, the wedding gazebo was swathed in fluffy white tulle, with fragrant lily of the valley and ferns adding a touch of color and scent. Here the couple would say their vows.

Of course the aunts knew someone who knew someone, and a stringed quartet softly played in one corner, the lovely strains of Beethoven filling the mountain air.

When everything was ready, Jake walked down the aisle and took his place at the gazebo entrance among his soon-to-be brothers-in-law, to wait for his bride.

"Excuse me, Jake," the pastor whispered.

"But is that cow with the, er, blue bow supposed to be there?"

"Yes." Jake stifled his laughter and explained. "Alexa wanted Sweetie nearby so she could watch. Don't worry. Sweetie's tied up."

"Okay then." The pastor cleared his throat as a signal to begin.

Gemma's nieces and nephews tromped down the aisle, scattering—actually throwing—rose petals. Alexa reminded Jake of Little Bo Peep as she tried to direct them, much like one would herd sheep. His soon-to-be daughter was thrilled with her fluffy blue party dress and new white shoes and she made sure everyone noticed them.

Once the children were seated on the turf on either side of the gazebo, Victoria led the walk toward Jake, followed by Adele and then Olivia. Beside their handsome husbands, the ladies looked beautifully elegant in their floaty summer-blue dresses, which were perfect, Gemma had assured him, for a casual summer wedding.

Jake could hardly wait to see her.

At a signal from the pastor, the quartet launched into the wedding song just as Gemma emerged from a nearby white tent. Aunt Tillie and Aunt Margaret walked with her on either side, their hands looped through her elbows. Their faces glowed with pride and love.

Jake caught his breath.

Gemma was stunning in a simple ankle-length white chiffon sundress that swirled and billowed around her sandaled feet in the warm summer breeze. She carried the wildflowers some of The Haven's guest children had found in the woods earlier this morning. Her long hair had been drawn off her face by a band of pearls and left to cascade down her back in a wash of auburn beauty. Sweet Gemma. She made his heart stop.

When the threesome reached Jake, the

aunts passed her hand to his, their smiles beaming through the tears filling their eyes.

"We love you both," Margaret whispered.

"So does God," Tillie added.

After sweet embraces, the ladies took their seats in the front row, next to Billy and Ethel who now claimed the title of matchmakers by assuring the entire town of Chokecherry Hollow that they'd brought Gemma and Jake together.

"You're beautiful, Gem," Jake murmured for Gemma's ears alone. "I love you."

"I love you, Jake."

There, among those who'd watched them overcome doubt and heartache, the couple said their vows, promising to love each other for the rest of their lives and to serve God in whatever path He directed. They sealed their promises with a kiss that seemed far too brief to Jake, though Alexa disagreed.

"How come it always takes 'em so long for kissin', Aunt Tillie?"

The pastor cleared his throat.

"At the couple's request, I will now read the twenty-third Psalm." The pastor began the familiar words. "'The Lord is my Shepherd...'"

Jehovah Raah. Another of God's names. Gemma smiled at Jake. Together they'd follow their shepherd wherever He led.

"Fellow guests, it is my honor to present to you, Mr. and Mrs. Elliot."

Gemma and Jake walked down the aisle, hands clasped, hearts locked, ready to enjoy this day and their future. Together.

Just before they left for their honeymoon, Tillie and Margaret gathered their family together.

"Isn't it just like God to give us The Haven to use for His work and then to bring all of our dear girls home and provide husbands who are perfectly equipped to help us carry on The Haven's ministries?" Margaret said.

"It's the best legacy we could pass on," Tillie agreed tearfully.

Later, Jake and Gemma were showered with rice as he helped her into his truck.

"For we know that all things work together for good for those who are called according to His purpose," Jake recited as he drove away. "We are being made into the image of His son. I get it now. This is our haven, too. Right, Gem?"

"I've traveled all over the world, but The Haven's where I belong, my darling," she agreed. "With you."

* * * * *

*If you enjoyed this story, pick up the other
Rocky Mountain Haven books.*

Meant-To-Be Baby
Mistletoe Twins
Rocky Mountain Daddy

And these other stories from Lois Richer:

The Rancher's Family Wish
Her Christmas Family Wish
The Cowboy's Easter Family Wish
The Twins' Family Wish
A Dad for Her Twins
Rancher Daddy
Gift-Wrapped Family
Accidental Dad

*Available now from Love Inspired!
Find more great reads at
www.LoveInspired.com.*

Dear Reader,

Thank you for returning to The Haven. I hope you enjoyed Gemma's and Jake's journeys to discover that God's plan is to help us become more like His son.

This was a difficult story to write. Losing that special person in your life is a heart-wrenching road to travel. There can be plenty of roadblocks to recovery when we demand explanations from God. While your heart aches with loss, your soul cries out for reasons why. Not getting them can either shut us down or drive us to overcome and move on to discover His plan. To do that, we must trust.

I'd love to hear from you. Please contact me via my website www.loisricher.com, on Facebook, at loisricher@gmail.com or at Box 639, Nipawin, Sk. Canada. S0E 1E0. I'll do my best to respond quickly.

Until we meet again, I wish you the blessing of a full heart that has not only known but given love, the joy of enriching some-one's world just by having you in it and the peace that comes from accepting that whatever happens, He has it under control.

Blessings,

Lois
Richer